THOSE THREE WORDS

AF433745

Those Three Words

Monica Marks

Published by Trellis Publishing, 2021.

This is a work of fiction. Similarities to real people, places, or events are entirely coincidental.

THOSE THREE WORDS

First edition. July 2, 2021.

Copyright © 2021 Monica Marks.

ISBN: 979-8224966349

Written by Monica Marks.

MONICA MARKS

She stared around the restaurant, her heart pounding. She was sure her face reflected the warm flush which had started in her belly and crept up her back toward the base of her pale neck. She had never been inside the five-star establishment and it was everything she had envisioned in her mind's eye.

I should have worn my hair down, Jannah thought as her hand nervously touched her throat. She knew she looked beautiful in the candlelight. The swoop neck evening gown was forest green and made her emerald colored eyes pop against her smooth skin and black hair. She hoped that Robert would not be able to take his eyes off her and so far, she had been successful in keeping his attention. His brown eyes sparkled in the shadows and he leaned in toward her.

This is it! She thought excitedly, reaching out to grasp his outstretched palms, trying to seek out where he had hidden the ring box. *It has been five insanely long years but he is finally ready to take the plunge. Oh, Lord, I hope I don't faint before he asks me.*

She tried to steady her breath and squeezed his hands affectionately.

"You look absolutely ravishing," Robert told her, his eyes shiny with adoration. "Every time I look at you, my heart skips a beat."

Jannah swallowed the lump in her throat. Their relationship had not always been seamless but even after all their time together, she was touched to know she still inspired a childlike wonder in him.

We love each other and that's all that matters. And to think that just last week you were thinking about ending things. Good thing you didn't take Lindsey's advice.

"Sometimes you've got to cut your losses and walk away," her best friend had said. "He might be the nicest guy in the world but if he's not giving you what you need out of life..."

Robert was building up to this all along. I couldn't rush things. He had to do them on his own terms. I'm glad I waited.

"Jannah, we've been together since senior year and I think we're the only ones of our friends who can claim anything like that," Robert told her. She nodded eagerly, blinking quickly so he would not see the tears in her eyes.

Your make-up is flawless right now. Don't let him propose to you with raccoon eyes!

"I know you've been wanting us to take the next step for a while now." Jannah found herself bristling as his words.

I've been wanting? What about you? She wondered, pulling back slightly. Robert did not seem to notice and he continued his obviously rehearsed speech.

Don't interrupt him. He doesn't always have a way with words. Let him finish.

"I want you to know I've picked up on all the hints you've dropped," he was saying and Jannah's warm blush turned icy cold. She felt her lids narrow so that her green eyes were barely visible between the slits.

Are you doing this because I've been hounding you or because you want to spend the rest of your life with me?

"And I'm ready to take the next step," he concluded, grinning like a small boy who had remembered all the lines in his school play. By this point, Jannah had flopped against the high back leather chair, her curvy arms folded against her full chest. He stared at her imploringly.

"What do you say, honey? Are you ready to take the leap with me?"

Jannah ground her teeth together and waited.

Don't get mad. Give him a chance. Romance is not his forte. Don't get mad...

"Jannah?"

"Aren't you even going to get down on one knee? Produce a ring?" she finally asked in disbelief as he stared at her. His mouth dropped open in shock and suddenly extended his arms as if to ward off a dangerous animal.

"Oh!" he gasped, his hand flying to his mouth. "Oh, no, no no!"

"No what?" she asked from between her clenched jaw. "No, you changed your mind? Or no, you're afraid you're going to throw out your back?"

"Oh, honey, the next step isn't marriage."

Jannah stared at her boyfriend like he had sprouted a second head.

"What is it then?" she hissed angrily. "What other leap is there?"

She found she was trembling.

Now he is just toying with my emotions. This is unbelievable.

"I was asking you to move in with me," he answered, his face suddenly turning ashen. Flabbergasted, Jannah glared, enraged at him. It took every ounce of willpower not to throw her glass of water in his face.

"Why on earth would you think that's what I would want?" she asked. Suddenly she wasn't furious but broken and she felt the energy in her body seep out of her body and under the white linen table cloth. All fight she had been harvesting flew far away from her. She was done.

He doesn't know me at all. How could he think that I would ever agree to move in with him after this amount of time? Has he ever really known me?

As she regarded Robert's confused and oblivious face, Jannah slowly rose to her feet. She felt very small despite her high heeled sandals.

"Where are you going, Jannah?" Robert demanded, rising to join her. She shook her head and gestured for him to sit.

"I'm doing what I should have done three years ago. Cutting my losses and walking away."

"Seriously? Are you sure?" Lindsey stopped walking and stared at Jannah in awe. Jannah nodded quickly before she could change her mind.

"Yes, but be quick about it," Jannah replied, continuing to walk down Main Street. "I don't want to have a chance to have cold feet."

"Oh, I'll be so quick, your head will spin," Lindsey squealed happily. "He's right in here."

Lindsey paused before the Middleton Methodist Church and started up the steps.

"Wait, what?"

Lindsey had been bugging her for weeks to start dating again even though Jannah had made it abundantly clear that she had been ruined by Robert's insensitive proposition.

"You must stop wallowing and seize opportunity when it strikes!" Lindsey had argued over the phone during one of their late-night talks. "I have the perfect man for you. If you two don't hit it off, it is because you're both sleeping. Trust me, he is your match! I knew if from the first time I met him."

It was odd; Jannah was not as depressed as she had anticipated as if deep down, she had known to expect this from Robert. She simply felt as if she had wasted so much time and energy holding onto something that was never going to happen.

On one hand, she knew Lindsey was right. She shouldn't waste another moment on Robert.

He has already claimed five years of your life. Don't give him the benefit of another second.

Another part of her wondered if her high school sweetheart would come to his senses and run back with his tail between his legs.

Who are you kidding? If he couldn't get it together in five years, he isn't going to do it now. And if he does, he's going to do it out of guilt, not because he wants to marry you. And what kind of life will that be? How will you sleep at night knowing you trapped someone into marriage?

She made her decision.

"I'd like to meet your perfect man for me," she told Lindsey as they left the hair salon. It had been Lindsey's idea, a girl's day at the spa and lunch afterward. Jannah knew that Lindsey had been worried about her since she had broken things off with Robert. To put Lindsey's mind at ease, Jannah had taken the day off work and joined Lindsey for an afternoon of pampering.

They were freshly polished and washed, smelling of honey and vanilla and Jannah had to admit that there was a spring in her step which hadn't been there before.

Lindsey is a good friend. She always knows just what to do. I should trust her, Jannah thought as they climbed the steps. Still, she could not shake the feeling of uneasiness which embraced her as they toward the majestic structure. It was the oldest building in their town and it loomed against the sky, easily the tallest construction for miles away but the size has little to do discomfort she felt.

"Why is he in church on a Friday?" Jannah asked as Lindsey pulled open the heavy wooden door. She smiled innocently, turning her light brown eyes on Jannah.

"Didn't I tell you? He's taking over for Pastor Giles next month when the Pastor retires."

"He's the new Reverend?" Jannah asked, freezing in her tracks. Her nerves were thinning more with each word Lindsey spoke.

She began to shake her head as the anxiety settled in her gut.

"No, wait, I changed my mind – "

"Nope, it's too late," Lindsey interrupted, yanking her unceremoniously by the arm and into the interior. There was no one inside the stoic walls, only rows of empty pews.

"See? No one's here. Let's go."

A feeling of apprehension stole over Jannah and the urge to flee was almost insurmountable.

"Wait a second, Miss Nervous Pants," Lindsey laughed, clasping Jannah's hand as if she was afraid the brunette would flee. "Let's see if he's in the office first. I would hate for us to miss him. It was like fate, you agreeing to meet him directly in front of the church, don't you think?"

Jannah smiled weakly and allowed Lindsey to lead her toward the back.

More like a bad omen, Jannah thought but she did not voice her doubt.

They passed the altar and made their way into the rear of the building when suddenly, they heard loud voices. Lindsey slowed her gait and the women regarded one another uncertainly. The shouting grew more intense as they made their way toward the ajar door.

"No, Elmer, I do no owe you anything! Once you retire, you are done with this church, do you hear me? I don't want your advice, your consultations – "

"You ungrateful fool!" Pastor Giles yelled back. "If not for me, you wouldn't have a position in this town to begin with! Show a little gratitude!"

"You make it very difficult to do that, Elmer. After next month, I suggest you keep a very low profile around these parts if you know what's good for you!"

Suddenly, the door to the office flung inward and a tall, blonde man stormed from the room, his face ablaze with anger. He froze when he saw Lindsey and Jannah.

"Hi Gavin..." Lindsey faltered. He stared blankly at her and then pushed past them, leaving the church through the front doors. Seconds later, Pastor Giles appeared in the doorway looking flustered.

"Ladies!" he called with forced cheer. "How long were you standing there?"

"Long enough," Lindsey mumbled, looking embarrassed but Pastor Giles patted her warmly on the shoulder. "What was that all about?"

"I'm sorry you had to witness that," he told them softly. "It seems like Pastor Stevens and I have a slight difference of opinion on some things."

Lindsey started to follow Pastor Giles into the back room but Jannah stood in her place, her eyes darting back toward the exit. She desperately wanted to follow in Pastor Stevens footsteps and leave the church in his wake.

"It sounded like more than a difference of opinion," Jannah muttered, averting her eyes from the reverend.

"Yes well, church business can be complicated," Pastor Giles replied smoothly. "And heated sometimes. What brings you ladies here? I don't think I've seen you inside these walls in years, Jannah!"

"I brought Jannah to meet Pastor Stevens but I can see that isn't going to happen today," Lindsey replied lightly, turning to her friend. "But maybe we'll meet him at Sunday service."

"He will certainly be here," the reverend replied. "And most likely in a calmer form."

He chuckled to take the edge from his words but Jannah caught a note of stress in his voice.

What kind of man orders the former pastor out of his own church? Jannah wondered as they left the building. She found herself looking upward at the cotton candy clouds in the sky.

Maybe the kind of man who knows what kind of man Pastor Giles is, she thought and ran to catch up with Lindsey before the memories threatening to flood her broke through.

"Honey, you're coming to church?" Jannah's mother looked shocked as her only daughter descended the stairs in a beautiful yellow and white sundress. Jannah's younger brother, Mason looked up from tying his shoe to give her a big smile.

"See mom? I told you that she would come with us one day. God told her it was time to come back," Mason informed their mother. Anne laughed and nodded.

"Well when God speaks, we all must listen, right, Jannah?"

Jannah forced a smile on her lips and bobbed her head in agreement. Church was still a very important aspect of her family's life but over the years, Jannah had not attended. When asked why by her brother or mother, she had a litany of excuses until finally they simply stopped asking. She wasn't sure why she had agreed to attend that day either but she suspected it was only to get a proper look of Gavin Stevens. She was not looking forward to the event but she tried to focus on Lindsey's sworn match.

He may not be my perfect mate but he has piqued my curiosity enough that I want a proper look at him. From what I caught of him whizzing by, he certainly seems attractive. Anyway, you promised Lindsey.

"Hurry up, Jannah." Mason stared up at her with eyes so much like hers. "Or are you intending to stand here until church is over?"

She accepted his extended hand and walked out into the warm summer sunshine.

"It is wonderful that you're coming with us," Anne whispered in her ear as they strolled down their tree-lined street. "I am so glad to see you coming around."

Jannah did not answer but she was already regretting her decision. A familiar sense of nausea was wracking her body as they drew nearer to the service and Jannah resisted the sudden urge to flee.

You can meet Gavin Stevens another time, she reasoned but her mother's arm tightened around hers as if sensing her reluctance.

As they turned the corner onto Main Street, Jannah could already see people milling out in front of the church, chattering pleasantly to one another. Lindsey was among the group and she smiled broadly when she caught sight of her best friend.

"There you are!" she declared, rushing forward to join the family. "I was worried you wouldn't come."

"When have I ever broken a promise to you?" Jannah retorted with more sharpness than she had intended. She didn't want her best friend to know she almost hadn't shown. Lindsey grinned.

"Never and I'm glad you didn't start today. Come on. Gavin is over there." She gestured toward the church steps and Jannah inhaled as if preparing herself for battle.

True to her word, Lindsey found Gavin on the stairs. Unlike the last time she had seen him, he was smiling and joking with the parishioner, no sign of the rude, demanding man who had been arguing with Pastor Giles.

"Sorry to interrupt you, Gavin but this is my friend Jannah whom I was telling you about," Lindsey announced, blatantly butting into his conversation. The Becker twins scowled at the intrusion but Gavin's beam widened as he stared at Jannah.

"Ah, yes, the famous Jannah Winters. It's a pleasure to finally meet you," he said, offering his hand. Jannah reluctantly accepted it, studying his face. His eyes were a warm blue like the depth of the Caribbean Sea and crinkled at the sides when he smiled. His hair was shiny and blonde but cut in a crew style, a flattering look for his wide, chiseled face. She could not detect an ounce of malice or arrogance in him and yet she could not help but think of the tone he used with Pastor Giles.

There are two sides to every story, she reminded herself. *You shouldn't jump to conclusions.*

Outwardly, she averted her eyes demurely. The Becker twins were still glaring daggers in her direction.

"I hope Lindsey hasn't been upselling me too much. I don't want to disappoint you," Jannah said lightly.

Gavin regarded her face intently, a soft expression on his face.

"I have a feeling that you would have a hard time disappointing me, Jannah."

It started as naturally as that. Gavin appeared on her doorstep on that Sunday evening and asked her out for a walk. Jannah had been touched by the simplicity of his offer.

Not, "Do you want to grab a coffee?" or "Want to see a movie?" but "Will you join me on a stroll?" It's so unpretentious and traditional. I can't ever imagine Robert asking me to take a walk.

That evening, they found their conversation flowing and unrushed. He had moved to Middleton from New York City, a fact which Jannah found fascinating.

"Why on earth would anyone move to Middleton, Illinois from the center of the universe?" she asked, staring at him in disbelief. Gavin had smiled kindly, providing his muscled forearm for him to take. For a moment, Jannah felt as if she was in a time warp, walking by the lake with the handsome pastor.

This is not something modern day adults do, she thought, relishing the feeling before she would be forced back into reality. Her whole life was too much realism and not enough imagination.

"New York City is not it's cracked up to be," Gavin told her enigmatically. "Plus, I much prefer living in a small town that a big city."

"Oh, so you've lived in small towns before," Jannah said, nodding understandingly.

"No, I was a New Yorker my whole life until I accepted this position," Gavin answered. Jannah arched a dark eyebrow in surprise.

"But you only just moved here. How can you tell you like it better here? I should be asking you in six months." He looked at her solemnly and Jannah felt a fusion of excitement course through her.

"I can just tell I like it here better," he replied, his blue eyes glittering.

They saw each other every night after work, if even for a short while. Each "date" was simple yet magical. There were hikes and light picnics, visits to the animal shelter to walk the dogs and rollerblading at the pier. And they talked. For hours upon hours about anything and everything.

"I have to admit, I am not a fan of set-ups, but Lindsey seemed awfully sure that you and I would hit it off," Gavin told her one evening. Jannah chuckled, recalling her own unwillingness to meet Gavin.

"She's got an old soul, that one," Jannah told him. "She seems to just inherently know things. I trust her judgement completely."

"She tells me that you just came out of a long-term relationship," he mentioned. Jannah cringed inwardly, wishing that Lindsey had not.

"Don't look so pained. I know Robert well enough. It would have come up in conversation," Gavin told her comfortingly. Jannah sighed and nodded.

"Yes, we were together for five years," she answered begrudgingly. Gavin's eyes seemed to widen with understanding.

"And he did not want to marry?"

"Apparently not," Jannah snapped and Gavin threw up his hands in mock surrender.

"I'm sorry if it's too personal. I am only trying to get to know you," he told her. Jannah immediately soften, a look of contrition passing over her face.

"I didn't mean to bite your head off," she told him apologetically. "It's just a sore subject. I guess I knew for a while that he wasn't the marrying type but instead of walking away, I stayed. I more feel like I wasted time than anything."

Gavin nodded thoughtfully and then smiled beguilingly at Jannah.

"Well I can tell you one thing for sure," he told her slowly.

"What's that?"

"You'll never have that problem with me."

"You won't waste my time?" she replied.

"You won't want to walk away," he answered seriously. Jannah lowered her head so he would not see the blush creeping into her cheeks.

It is so natural and comfortable with him, she thought. *I feel like we've known one another forever. Lindsey really did hit the nail on the head with him.*

"Why don't you attend church often?"

The question was unexpected and Jannah felt the hairs on the back of her neck rise in defensiveness.

"What do you mean?" she shot back. "I met you at the church."

Both times, she almost said. She had an inert desire to put him on the defensive in deflection by asking him about argument he had with Pastor Giles.

"Yes, I know that but you haven't been back since," Gavin replied gently. "I'm not judging you. I was just curious as to the reason. I won't be mad if you say you don't care for church."

Jannah bit the insides of her cheeks and steadied her suddenly pounding heart.

"I like church just fine but I get busy, just like everyone else," she lied. Gavin shrugged and nodded in agreement.

"It happens to the best of us," he told her. He opened his mouth to say something else but quickly changed his mind, clamping his lips together.

"What?" she demanded, the anger rushing back into her.

He has no right to question my attendance in church. He doesn't know me and he's judging my level of spirituality. I can speak to God anywhere. I don't have to go to service to do that. Just because he's the new pastor doesn't mean –

"I was just going to say that I will never force my desires on you but I certainly would love to look out from the pulpit and see your beautiful green eyes every Sunday morning."

Her annoyance dissipated like water on a hot sidewalk and her blush deepened.

"I will be there from now on," she murmured.

There is no need to be afraid of the church anymore, she told herself. *Pastor Giles will be gone soon too.*

"Things are going well with Pastor Stevens I take it?"

Lindsey's question was rhetorical but Jannah nodded confirmation.

"You certainly have an eye for matchmaking," she told her friend jokingly. "Maybe you should set up a service."

Lindsey's dark eyes twinkled mischievously and she shook her head.

"Nah, I'll stick to using my powers for good not for greed," she replied. Her face turned serious.

"You're spending more time in church now, huh?"

Jannah glanced nervously at her hands.

"Yep."

"Jannah look at me."

She glanced up at Lindsey's concerned face, bracing herself for a lecture.

"I don't know what happened all those years ago, but I'm glad you're letting your faith in God overcome whatever darkness you've been harboring."

Jannah gritted her teeth, tempted to spill the entire sordid story to Lindsey but she restrained herself.

"Gavin is helping me love the church again," she told Lindsey, forcing a smile onto her face. "It's difficult not to enjoy watching such a handsome reverend, am I right?"

Lindsey chuckled but Jannah could tell she was concerned.

"You know I am always here if you need someone to talk to, right?"

"Of course!" Jannah replied. "And the same goes for you."

The returned to their sandwiches, Jannah's eyes straying toward the exterior of the diner. Directly across the street loomed the dark building of worship. As always, the sight of the structure gave her shivers.

One day looking at that place won't upset me, she vowed. She wondered how long that would take.

Gavin slipped nicely into life in Middleton. He was easily welcomed into the community and he savored the politeness and decency of the people. It was the glaring opposite of the church he had come from in the Bronx. He never found homeless people sleeping on the steps, starving and cold. He was not subject to abuse or profanity by drug addicted parishioners. No one begged him for money to feed their children.

He had found himself questioning his faith daily. The human suffering and decay he had experienced through members of his church made him wonder why he was bothering.

If one is cured, there will be four more to take his place. It is never ending.

Finally, he had gone to the Council of Bishops to explain his plight.

"I don't think I can do this anymore," he had told them, spiritually and emotionally drained. "I am starting to question my faith."

There had been a general meeting, the council returning to him a few days later.

"Pastor Stevens, we have spoken at length about your situation and we feel that you should at least give your calling another chance before 'throwing in the towel' if you will."

Gavin had considered his words and agreed but there had been a warning attached.

"We are sending you to replace a retiring pastor," the president informed him. Gavin had shrugged.

"That sounds fine," he started to say but the lead of the council held up his hand.

"Pastor Giles is being forced into retirement," the president continued. Gavin felt his eyes narrow suspiciously.

"Why?"

"That is really not your concern at this time. However, if you should become aware of it at a later point, you are to maintain to the parish that Pastor Giles has retired. Do you understand?"

Slowly, Gavin had nodded but he did not understand at all. Until he had arrived in Middleton.

His rage had been overwhelming when he discovered the truth about Pastor Giles' retirement, returning to the Council of Bishops and demanding justice for the victims.

"It is too late now," the president had told him, sadly. "It is much too late for everyone involved."

Gavin had been forced to accept the feeble answer but it did not stop him from speaking his mind to Pastor Giles. He had been relieved that the Pastor had quietly left the church and not returned as Gavin had demanded.

He had also made the connection that with Pastor Giles gone, Jannah was suddenly less reluctant to attend worship.

She was one of the victims too, he realized with sick horror.

There was a horse and carriage sitting outside her house when Jannah returned home from work that evening. Dressed like a coachman from the 1800s, Gavin sat at the reins, smiling wickedly as she laughed.

"Where on earth did you get that?" she demanded.

"What? The top hat?"

"All of it!" She laughed again and hurried toward him so he could lift her onto the seat beside him.

"This is fantastic!" she announced as they rode down the street in the buggy. Their neighbors waved in amusement as they passed by.

"You are full of surprises," Jannah commented as they continued. She looked at him adoringly and he returned her gaze.

"Jannah, how old were you when it happened?" he asked. Jannah was confused at first.

"When what happened?" she asked, the smile still on her face.

"The first time he touched you."

Her blood ran cold and her face contorted into a look of shock.

"Who told you about that?" she hissed, looking around as if someone was eavesdropping on their conversation but of course there was only the horses within earshot.

"No one told me," he answered gently. "I figured it out myself."

Jannah folded her arms across her chest and looked out toward the lake. She had never spoken of it to anyone, not since it had happened fifteen years prior.

She had been ten years old, skipping around the near empty church between the pews when he called out to her.

"Hey Jannah! Can you help me? I seem to have dropped my glasses under the seat."

Without a second thought, Jannah made her way toward the front of the church and saw him on his knees, ducking his head underneath the benches.

"Oh, I can do it," she volunteered, not wanting to see him straining. Gratefully, he lifted himself onto the pew and exhaled heavily. Jannah crouched down to look for his spectacles and as she turned, she felt a calloused hand slip under her skirt. Yelping, she jumped up and stared at him in shock.

"What are you doing?" she demanded. She realized that his eyes were glassy and his other hand was in his pants, his breath rising and falling. His tongue jutted out and licked his lips and Jannah was sure she was going to vomit. Without turning around, she backed her way out of the pews, squeezing her eyes shut to block out what she was seeing. Backward she half ran and half walked until she collided with a figure.

"Jannah, you must watch where you're walking!" Pastor Giles told her as she spun to look at him. Without speaking she pointed at old Mr. Caspar who was still watching her, a twisted smile on his lips. Pastor Giles' mouth pursed into a fine line.

"Go home, Jannah," he told her quietly. "And say nothing of this to anyone. Promise me!"

"But Pastor – "

"Promise me!" Pastor Giles urged. "God will know if you're lying."

"I promise," she whispered, fearfully. She turned and fled the church, never looking back.

"Jannah, I understand this is difficult to speak about but it might help if you finally say it out loud."

"Why? You already know what happened. How could you know? Did Pastor Giles tell you?"

Gavin laughed mirthlessly.

"No. No he didn't..."

"Pastor Stevens, may I have a word with you?"

He glanced up and watched Mary-Anne Giles peek her head into the office.

"Of course, Mrs. Giles! Please come in." He gestured for her to sit but the pastor's wife paced about nervously.

"I am here completely off the record," she told him nervously. "If anyone finds out it was I who told you, well, I'm sure I don't have to tell you what will happen to me in a bible-belt town like Middleton."

"I assure you, Mrs. Giles that anything you say to me will be kept in the strictest of confidence." Mary-Anne sighed and sat laboriously into a chair facing the attractive newcomer.

"I am only here because I know that you are going to hear about it from someone else and I would rather you hear it from me because I know Elmer better than anyone in the world. He is not a bad man. He loves God and this community but he didn't know what to do."

"Okay, slow down, Mary-Anne. You need to take a deep breath and explain to me what happened."

Mary-Anne Giles inhaled deeply and turned her dark eyes toward Gavin.

"There was a man who belonged to this church," she began. Gavin nodded encouragingly.

"He molested children." Gavin cringed and tried to maintain his stoic expression but he could feel his face cracking. It never got easier to hear. No matter how many confessions he heard, how many counselling sessions he performed, how many prayer groups he hosted, words like those could not be unheard.

"That is a difficult burden to carry," Gavin told her softly. Elmer Giles was bound to an oath of privacy just as any other member of the clergy. He could not have turned the parishioner in despite the desire to do so.

"Is this man still a member of the church?" Gavin needed to know. Mary-Anne shook her head.

"He died recently which is why this has come to light. This man's victims are feeling safe enough to come forward now that he is gone. He often molested little girls in this very church…"

Gavin felt a dull thudding begin in his head.

"That is his sin, a sin only God can forgive. That is not Elmer's sin," Gavin choked, gritting his teeth.

He should have known what was happening in his own church! The young pastor thought but he still understood that it was not guilt which belonged to Pastor Giles.

"Elmer knew about it. He would walk in on it happening and send the girls on their way after swearing them to secrecy."

Gavin leapt to his feet before he could stop himself.

"He covered the deeds of a child predator in his own church?" he asked dubiously. If it had been anyone other than the pastor's own wife standing there, he would have second guessed the validity of what she was saying. The look in Mary-Anne's brown eyes told him that she was not lying.

He bears responsibility in this too! Gavin thought, furiously. His mind began to whirl as he thought of a way to ensure Elmer Giles faced justice.

"It doesn't matter. James Caspar is dead now and even if he wasn't, there's no way I could prove something that happened that long ago."

"You could if Elmer Giles has stepped forward when it happened," Gavin replied. He had no idea if Pastor Giles had witnessed Jannah's abuse but he took a shot to see if his hunch was right.

"He wouldn't do that. It would be a mark against his church and him. He would be scrutinized for not banishing such a monster in our midst."

Gavin was silent for a moment.

"There were other victims," he told her softly and she shrugged, blinking the tears from her eyes. "They can testify that Pastor Giles not only did nothing but covered up such an atrocity. It is not too late."

Jannah peered at him out of the corner of her eye.

"What will that accomplish?" she asked slowly.

"Maybe nothing," Gavin agreed, steering the horses toward the bank of the lake. He lowered the reins and looked at her.

"Maybe everything. You are not the only one who has suffered in silence, made to feel guilty and uncomfortable in a church of all places. James Caspar stole your sense of security but Pastor Giles held it hostage."

"What do you think I should do?" Jannah asked uncertainly.

"I think you and the other victims should go to the police and make a report. They will have counsellors you can speak with and they will make a decision as to whether or not they will pursue Pastor Giles for a crime."

"What if they don't?" Jannah wondered. "He will be furious. He might retaliate."

Gavin sighed and shook his head.

"Believe it or not, Jannah, I don't think he feels anything but shame for what he has done. I think he will repent to God and beg you for forgiveness."

Jannah pondered his words, her eyes still trained on the blue of the water.

This man has come from nowhere and brought me back into the church. I haven't wanted to step foot inside those doors in years. He believes that I can overcome this shame and fear. And I believe in him.

"I will make a statement," she decided and Gavin nodded, brushing a strand of hair from her face.

"Let me know when you're ready to do that. I will go with you," he told her tenderly.

"I want to go now," she surprised him by announcing.

"Now? Are you sure?"

She nodded. She did not want to wait another minute to let the weight she had been carrying off her shoulders.

Gavin nodded and picked up the reins, the horses snorting in protest. As they galloped away, Gavin smiled to himself and touched the ring box in his pocket.

She waited twenty-five years to meet me, fifteen years for justice and five years for marriage, he thought wryly. *I can wait five more hours to propose to her.*

DEEP IN THE AMISH HEART

MEGHAN MASON

Sarah's day began as any other. The sky was clear and blue with a scattering of pillow clouds, and Sarah was walking the two mile stretch between her home and her father's general store in town. Each morning she had to arise from her sleep before sunrise to fulfill all the household duties. There were chickens to be fed, produce to be picked, and breakfast to be prepared for herself, her daed, Jacob, and her two younger siblings. Sarah was the oldest, at seventeen, then came her schwester Hope at nine years old, and finally boppli bruder, Noah. Their maam had passed away during childbirth just a year ago next month. Noah had not even had his first birthday yet. In Amish life, this meant that Sarah, being the eldest daughter, was now responsible for keeping house and raising her younger siblings. It was an enormous responsibility, but one that Sarah did with a willing and loving heart. She loved to sing softly to herself as she dressed in her pale blue dress, white apron and bonnet. As she completed all the morning chores, Sarah liked to sing her favorite church hymns. It helped to make the chores go by faster, and always served to put her in a good mood.

Today, as Sarah made her way down the dirt path that led to town, she hummed a little tune, and thought about what a long day it would be for her working at her daed's store. She loved her father, but Jacob Williams was renowned in the small Amish community as a very strict task master. He could certainly be overbearing at times, but Sarah understood how difficult life had become for him since her mamm's death. Jacob had loved his wife, Elizabeth very much. They had married at only sixteen years old, and planned on making a life together as they grew in their love for one another into ripe old age. It was not Gott's will however, and now the Williams family had to adjust to life without mamm. Sarah knew her daed was lonely most times, and that that was what made him so domineering at times. It didn't make things any easier on Sarah, however, and taking care of the home, plus working at the store was exhausting. She did this all without complaint, and thanked Gott for her many blessings. The store sold local goods from the community farmers, and some of the women sewed items of clothing or household linens upon special request. Often, specific Englischers would place orders for tablecloths or various linens, and the ladies who had grown children, thus having extra time on their hands, would take up the task.

Sarah entered the store, and greeted her father in traditional Pennsylvania Dutch, as he was of the Old Order who still adhered strictly to Amish customs, "Guder Mariye, daed," she said cheerfully. As per usual, Jacob eyed his eldest daughter with a certain unfounded suspicion, but returned her morning greeting just the same.

"Sarah, there is much to accomplish today. You can start with sweeping and dusting the shelves, and then take over the accounts book. I need to go to see Farmer Pickens about eggs, since he is late with delivery," he stated. This was bound to be a long day, but if she was left alone in the store for most of the day, she could at least indulge herself in singing. Daed did not approve of Sarah's love of song outside of the religious environment or outside the home, as was the custom of her faith. Nonetheless, Sarah felt it to be a harmless enough past time if she wasn't running around town singing for everyone to hear. Jacob watched her as she retrieved the broom, and then he departed for Farmer Pickens'.

As Sarah swept the already very clean oak floors, she sang a lovely hymn from last Sunday's service. It was called, "The Lord Provides," and she loved it because of the sweet notes and fortifying lyrics. She was alone in the store, and she allowed herself to really sing out. Singing was the thing that made her feel the happiest, and soon enough she was in a world of her own.

Outside, a young man strolled along the road, thinking about how relieved he felt about having made the move to a simpler life in the country. He enjoyed the pristine air, and the beautiful woods, and had a healthy respect for the Amish community. The outlying farms and cottages that were not Amish, coexisted peacefully together, respecting one another's privacy and traditions. The town called Havensville was a perfect place to call home after the disaster he had left behind him in the big city of Pittsburgh. The young man was just eighteen, but mature enough to recognize the dysfunction of his family life. His father's alcoholism had been taking its toll on him and his mother for many years, and she had recently passed away from a lengthy battle with cancer. He tried to care for his father, but he would have none of it, and continued his wayward lifestyle. So, after much thought, he decided to leave school, where he was studying music, and start fresh somewhere new. The young man packed his bags, gathered what meager funds he had saved from after school jobs, and caught the next bus out to the countryside. He stopped short when he saw the quaint wooden store in front of him. It was painted a fresh white with simple blue trim, and had a small garden of wildflowers in the front. There was a cobblestone walkway leading up to the entry, and a hanging sign above the door that read, "William's General Store." Nothing flashy, but it was adorned with a little bluebird in the righthand corner of the square sign. The store looked like something out of a storybook with its flowers and front porch swing. He decided he should go in and stock up on supplies and grocery items since this was his very first day in town. He entered the store, and there he observed a modest, yet beautiful young woman singing her heart out as she dusted the many shelves behind the register. Her back was turned to him, and she had not noticed the bell as he had entered the store.

"Excuse me please, miss?"

Sarah gave a startled jump, as she whipped around. She felt embarrassed that she hadn't heard anyone enter the store, and here she was singing away!

"Oh, my goodness! I'm terribly sorry. I didn't hear you come in, sir," Sarah replied.

"It is not a problem. I quite enjoyed your song. You have a lovely singing voice," the young man said. Sarah blushed crimson at his compliment, as she was shy towards strangers, and she had not seen this young man around the village area,

"How may I help you, Mr....." Sarah inquired.

"I am hardly worthy of the title of Mr., but my name is John Anders, and I have only just arrived here in Havensville this early morning," He replied. Sarah thought him a fine-looking man, around her own age, but wondered why on earth he had come here to live in such a small and isolated place, "Where are you coming from, Mr. Anders? And you are with your family, I presume?"

"No, I am here alone from Pittsburgh. It was time for me to start a new life of my own. This place seemed good enough as any other, I guess," offered John, "and please, call me John, and may I ask your name?"

"Ok, my name is Sarah, and my father owns the store. Alright then, John, what would you like?" Sarah began to list what sundries and groceries the simple store offered, but John stopped her, and said he was here for basic living supplies, like food and a few other items such as general toiletries,

"Miss Sarah, I guess I would be grateful if you just took charge and filled my basket with whatever cooking things you think best, and I'll go in search of my personal items?" said John hopefully, as he was not at all knowledgeable about what exactly he would need.

As Sarah made up a large basket of fruits, vegetables, and other things she thought necessary for a young bachelor, John returned to the counter with another basket filled with such items as a hairbrush, toothbrush, toothpaste, sponges, and other assorted things. John thought Sarah was delightful, friendly and kind, and decided to ask her a few questions about Havensville,

"Sarah, thank you for helping me sort out all these things! You are such a help, because this is honestly the first time I have ever been out on my own, and I haven't the slightest clue what I'm planning to do. I do not even have anywhere to stay yet, or any prospects of a job. Do you happen to know of anywhere that may offer a room, and perhaps some honest work?"

Sarah studied John, and figured since he had a gentle looking face and good manners, that she really should help welcome the new comer to his new home. She thought hard for a moment or two, and then replied,

"I know Farmer Pickens has been late with his egg deliveries lately, now that his Betty has had their boppli, oh! I mean baby..." she stammered, remembering that John was likely unfamiliar with their ways of speaking, but without skipping a beat, John said,

"No, please Sarah, use your traditional words. I took the liberty of reading up on Amish tradition and life during the bus ride. I am proud to say that I think I now am familiar with many unfamiliar words!" Sarah was surprised at John's eagerness and willingness to learn some Pennsylvania Dutch, and this only made him more attractive in her eyes.

"Anyways, John, I was going to say that Farmer Pickens might have some dairy work for you, and my daed may like to have a helper with building the new barn at home. He's out at Pickens place, now, but should be returning within the hour," Sarah volunteered. For am Englischer, John Anders was certainly a nice young man, and she was impressed with his independence and desire to fit into the small community.

John smiled, as he paid for his groceries, while Sarah bagged them in plain paper sacks. He was going to have his hands full with these many bags, but he could make it to wherever he was going just fine. He just had to figure out just where it was he was going, and he decided to engage Sarah in more conversation, "Well, perhaps I should wait outside then for your father to return, so that I can sort out some work. I have nowhere in particular to go just now, so I guess your front porch swing is as good a place as any to pass the time." His simple manner made Sarah smile again, and she said he was welcome to the swing while she finished up her duties inside.

"Perhaps you would care for some homemade lemonade when I am finished?" Sarah offered.

"Yes, that sounds wonderful, Sarah. Thank you, kindly! Will you join me then, once you're finished?" he asked hopefully. Again, Sarah blushed, but she did agree to sit awhile on the swing until her father returned, if no other customer came calling. John went outside, and Sarah hurriedly went back to her dusting.

Once outside, John scanned the pretty little porch, and sat down on the swing. It was of fine craftsmanship, and constructed from a sturdy pine, he thought. He sat there quietly thinking that he had made an excellent choice in coming to this place. If everyone was as nice as Sarah Williams, then he was sure to feel at home. Now he just had to find a place to live. He felt a bit nervous, since it was approaching afternoon, and he did not want to be homeless on his first night in a new town. As John was busy fretting about what to do next, Sarah had finished her work, and was preparing a tray of iced cold lemonade. She thought he might be hungry after his long bus journey, and so she made up a plate of sandwiches and sliced some fresh peaches from her own orchard. She had brought them as part of her own midday meal, but felt it would be nice to share with John. She liked the idea of sitting out front with the young man, even though father would probably not approve of her sitting alone with a stranger. She carried the tray outside, and noticed the look of obvious concern on John's face.

"Whatever is the matter, John?" as she placed the lunch things on the side table. John looked thankfully at her, and said,

"Sarah, you certainly did not have to go to such trouble on my account! Thank you. I do feel hungry. To tell you the truth, I am concerned about where I might find lodging for tonight. I am sure I can find something more permanent as I become more familiar with the folks in town," John confided.

"Don't you worry just yet," she reassured him, and poured him a nice glass of lemonade. She placed a sandwich in his lap, and began to make pleasant conversation about the weather, and who was who in town, and so on...John couldn't help but recall her beautiful singing voice when he had first entered the store. She had such a lovely voice! He could think of nothing more wonderful than to hear her singing again, as he missed his music studies, and was a decent singer himself, but he knew he must not seem to forward. He hoped he might someday hear her angelic voice again, as he got to know her better, and realized he was lost in his daydreams of her, as she chattered on. He forced himself back to reality, and listened to everything she was saying regarding life in and around the town. The care she had taken making him sandwiches and sharing the juicy peaches did not go unnoticed. He could not have wished for a lovelier welcome.

Just after a half hour or so, Jacob's horse drawn buggy was making its way towards the store front. Sarah could already see his tense looking eyes, and frowny expression, as he noted that his daughter was sitting unattended with a strange young newcomer. He parked the buggy hastily, and walked briskly up the front steps to the swing,

"What have we here, Sarah? Why are you not minding the store?" he demanded.

"Daed, please welcome Mr. John Anders from Pittsburgh. He has travelled here by bus to make a life for himself, and came in to purchase his necessities," announced his daughter. Jacob stared at the young Englischer with some uneasiness, as he was always wary of outsiders. You never knew how they would take to the Amish customs, after all. Nonetheless, Jacob was not to be a rude man, so he extended his hand in greeting,

"Kannscht du Pennsilfaanisch Deitsch schetzer?" blurted Jacob, knowing full well that Mr. Anders certainly did not speak Pennsylvania Dutch. It was Jacob's way of distancing himself from the young stranger, and he was obviously annoyed that Sarah had engaged him in conversation, and then apparently fed him as well! A little too welcoming, he thought to himself.

"Uh, no, I think what you said was 'Do I speak Pennsylvania Dutch? I confess I am not very familiar with it as of yet, but did have a chance to study some on my way here. I am a quick study, luckily, and hope to pick up the language here and there," John returned quickly. He could understand a father's protective nature, and realized he was the new person in town, so he had better do his best to make a proper first impression,

"It is good to meet you, Mr. Williams," said John, and then Sarah thankfully took over and explained that he was in search of some steady work, and a place to cover his head.

Jacob's predictable answer to this announcement was, "Englischers! Sie scheie sich vun haddiArewat." John made out at least some of what was said, and promptly and wisely replied, "No sir, I am a hard worker, and am willing to take on anything that is available. I need to learn to make my own way in the world now that I am my own man. I can assure you I am a man of my word, and an honest worker for anyone who needs help. I studied music, but am not afraid of a man's work in the fields or building. Whatever needs to be done, I will do it, and I will do it well," promised John Anders. Jacob had to admit that he approved of the boy's answer, though he was no boy, but rather a young man of about eighteen to twenty years of age. As much as he would have preferred otherwise, Jacob knew he needed help building the barn that was to house the new horses, goats, and cows. They were due in for delivery from the neighboring town of Lancaster in three weeks' time, and he would never finish the job alone,

"Tell you what, young Mr. Anders. I need a strong young man to build my barn with me. I'll need ya to be schmaert (smart) and no schlofkopp (sleepyhead)! I'll give ya board in the shack out back. Sarah will make it home for ya, and put some extra furnishings in there. It'll be small, but I imagine it's a darn sight better than nothing.," and as Jacob had finished his little speech and offer of work and board, John couldn't help but smile wide! This was just perfect, and exactly what he needed, which was not much. Just somewhere to call home, and a place where he could lay his head at night after a hard day's work, "Many thanks, sir! I am much obliged to you for your kind and generous offer." Sarah could only stare blankly at her father's unexpected good nature, and she couldn't help but feel a surge of excitement that John, whom she now considered a friend, would be staying right there on their farm! It would no doubt mean one more mouth to cook and clean for, but she was happy to have the friendly John join her little clan. She enjoyed her household duties, and one more surely would not be any bother.

Jacob said, "Mr. Anders, you wait here till closing time, and we'll go home in the buggy, and get you situated. Sarah, you will have extra work tonight getting Mr. Anders settled and preparing the meal. I expect a satisfying meal, so go on home and get started early then! No time to be standing around on the porch making idle talk," and so he dismissed Sarah, and off she went back home to give that shack a thorough cleaning. By now, Hope would be home from her book learning, and together they could muster what strength they had, and drag some extra furnishings into John's new home. It would take some effort to make that old shack into a home, but she would do it happily for John.

As evening fell, Sarah and Hope had just put the finishing touches on John's new abode, when the buggy arrived. The two men got out, and she noticed that John had not cases or trunk. That meant he had only the clothes on his back! She would start to sewing him some pants and shirts just as soon as she could. But now, there was a beef stew to get on the table for supper, and children to wash up. She practically ran back to the house to check on her stew, and slice the bread. Her father would want dinner on the table straight away.

"Welcome to our home," said Sarah, and she introduced him to each member of the family, including boppli, Noah, and then served up the stew. Everyone enjoyed pleasant conversation, though Jacob kept fairly quiet. He was not one for conversation. Sarah noticed that John ate his supper and hoped that he had had enough to eat. She offered homemade apple tart for dessert, "Sarah, I must thank you for your family's hospitality. I must admit I heard you singing earlier this afternoon in the store! You have an exceptional voice, if you don't mind my saying so. Do you sing at church service? You should not deprive the rest of the town of such a heavenly sound. Do you think you'll sing at the Town Square Picnic your father was telling me about on the way home?" Jacob let his fork drop with a clatter, and John suspected he had somehow misspoke,

"I will have you know, Mr. Anders, that we Amish do not sing for personal glory. Sarah will sing at service only; do you hear that maedel!" spat her father. Sarah already knew how her father felt about her love for singing, and couldn't help but feel sorry for the way John must feel at her father's reproach. Sarah nodded in agreement, and quietly resumed eating her apple tart. When dinner was finished, she cleared the table, and washed up the dishes. Meanwhile, Jacob had taken John out to survey the barn building, and explain what was needed in the coming three weeks. It was going to be a stretch, thought John, to get that barn built in time for the animals, but a promise was a promise. He'd get the job done mostly on his own while Jacob was working at the store. Then they would work on it together till dark in the weeks to come.

John made his way to his meager home, but upon entering the front door, he was amazed at what a spectacular job Sarah had done sprucing the place up! The wooden floors gleamed and smelled like fresh soap, and she had put pretty little curtains up around the window. He felt badly that she had been put to such trouble dragging in furniture, but was relieved to see it was just a simple chair and table, a cot made up into a comfy looking bed. She had supplied him with lots of fluffy blankets and a pillow, and there was a plain white porcelain ewer and basin for washing. It was perfect! Simple and comfortable was all he wanted or needed. He felt a strange stirring in his heart that Sarah was the one who had taken such care in setting up his new home. He definitely liked her very much, and looked forward to seeing her at meal times and whenever else he could squeeze in a moment with her. He wondered what she thought of him, and the sound of her singing filled his head as he fell asleep that night.

The next few days passed by with plenty of work on the barn. In fact, Sarah and the others only saw the menfolk at meals. She had to admit to herself that she missed talking with John. Her father retired earlier than normal that night directly after supper, and John was nice enough to help wash up. She offered him a hot cup of rose-hip tea by the fireside, as she readied Hope and Noah for bedtime. With the younger ones fast asleep, she joined John in the main room. She had been softly singing a good night song for the children, and he had listened with great joy from his chair by the fire,

"Sarah, I wanted to say thank you for making me so at home. I love being here, and sharing life with your family. Sure, your father may be a bit brusque, but he means well, and is very protective of you as a father should be. I couldn't help but overhear your singing the children to sleep. It was very beautiful. I would be honored to come to service to hear you sing if I may? Am I allowed as an outsider to attend?" he inquired.

"Yes, John, all are welcome. You will be seated on one side, along with all the other single men. You will fit in, because they do not yet have beards. Those are for the married men only," she giggled slightly as she imagined John taking part in the Amish service. It rotated from house to house every Sunday, "My father will like that you are wanting to attend our service. He will be impressed, and I already know that he values all your arduous work. He told me so just yesterday morning as he left for the general store," confided Sarah. John had been working double time to make certain that the barn would be ready on time. He also hoped Mr. Williams might need him to care for the animals, since he was responsible for tending the store. John would like to stay on, sharing in their lives, and he would be willing to learn how to tend to the animals and any farm work for her father. It was getting late, and John stood to make his way across the yard to his room. "Sarah," he asked nervously, "Would it be appropriate for you to walk with me to the shack?"

"Well, father is asleep, so I do not see any problem with that," she agreed tentatively. She had grown to really admire John, and hoped he would stay on and perhaps be happy here. But, she knew that he was an Englischer, and would always remain an outsider. She also knew that she could never entertain the idea of him courting her, as she was expected to court an Amish man. It was time for her to be looking for her own husband, as she was of age, and this was the Amish tradition. She put the thought out of her mind, and got up to walk John back to his tiny home.

As they walked together, John looked up at the starry sky, and commented on the cool night, "Are you warm enough, Sarah? If not, please take my coat," as he noticed her shiver in the moonlight. He loved the way she always blushed in his presence. He hoped that Sarah felt for him as much as he felt for her. For he was already falling in love with her, but knew he must tread very carefully, in order to keep Jacob a happy and trusting man.

"Would you sing a hymn for me, Sarah?" asked John, as he looked at her by the starlight, "It is allowed if it is a hymn, honoring Gott, as you say," and they grinned at his use of the Amish expression.

"I guess it would be ok," she said, and she chose the very same song that she had been singing that day he entered the general store. John listened to every lilt of her voice, and suppressed his urge to kiss her. That would have been too soon, and he was determined to make no gestures that she may not expect, though he sensed she might be hoping for the same thing. However, there was the issue of John not being part of the Amish faith, and this was going to present a huge problem if he were to act upon his feelings. He couldn't help but take her hand in his as they reached his door. Sarah stopped her song rather abruptly, and shied away from John immediately. He felt he had blundered the moment, but she did not run off,

"I am sorry to make you uncomfortable, Sarah. It's just that you sing so beautifully and sweetly, that it fills my heart with such happiness. I understand that I am not of your faith, but there is something I must speak to your father about before the end of the month. I am considering joining the Amish in life and in faith. I want to be worthy of your affections, as you must have guessed by now, my dear little songbird. I cannot bear not to hear your lovely singing. It is too bad that the Amish do not allow singing for secular purposes, but I can understand why."

Sarah stood somewhat aghast at John's admission of love, though she returned his feelings wholeheartedly. She would like nothing so much in this world as to be able to love John, but there were obvious hurdles that would have to be addressed, "John, it is very uncommon for an outsider to join the Amish ways, but it is not unheard of. We have never had one in our small community, but I have heard tale of it in larger ones," she stated confidently. Did she dare allow herself to love him back? This was a question that would have to wait. They said their good nights, and John watched as she got to her front door safely. John was more than a little intimidated at the thought of having to discuss becoming Amish with Jacob. He resolved to have that conversation before this Sunday. With that settled in his mind, John fell to sleep, and dreamed a beautiful dream of Sarah running through the meadow singing for all of nature and Gott to hear.

Over the next few days, John waited for an opportune time to broach the subject of his intentions to join the Amish. After working a bit later than usual, John and Jacob finally sat down upon the workbench, and John tried his best to engage Jacob in normal pleasantries. After a short while, John decided to tell Jacob what he wished to do,

"Mr. Williams, sir, I have treasured my time here working with you, and living side by side with your wonderful family. There is something very important that I wish to speak with you about."

"Yes, John, what is this that you need to discuss at this late hour?" replied Jacob.

"I understand that we are both very tired, and the hour is rather late, but this is something that is weighing heavily upon my mind, and something that I must speak with you about, and I prefer that we do so alone," offered John.

"Alright, then. Out with it. What is so important, John?"

"I have given this much thought, and I admire your way of life, and the way that your faith enters into every aspect of life. I have noticed how it makes me feel closer to Gott, and I want to join the faith. I realize that this is a rarity, but it is all that I want. You are an intelligent and observant man, Mr. Williams, and you must have noticed my affection for your lovely Sarah. I know that I cannot ask for her hand unless I am an Amish man. I seek to enter the Amish religion not just for the sake of Sarah, but for my own well-being. I want to fully belong to this community, and I want to worship and live just as you do," said John with as much earnestness as he could muster.

"Mr. Anders, though your intentions seem true and honest to me, you are correct in thinking that an Englischer cannot possibly enter into marriage with my daughter. I will speak to the men of the church before Sunday, but I must warn you that you are about to take on a long and serious obligation to Gott," answered Jacob, much to John's relief. This answer was what he was desperately hoping to hear from Sarah's father. It was proof, however small, that he accepted John as a suitor for Sarah once he converted to the Amish faith. It was something important he would be doing for himself and for Sarah. He had been practicing something special for Jacob, and now seemed the perfect time to say it. John stood up, and without further ado, launched into the Pennsylvania Dutch phrase he had been studying since he arrived. For it was on that very day, that John already knew that he must win the love of Sarah if he was ever to be a happy man,

"Mer sott em sei Eagne net verlosse; Gott verlosst die Seine night," and that is what John said right then and there to Jacob, which translated to "One should not abandon one's own; God does not abandon his own."

Jacob looked like the most surprised man on the face of the earth. Not only had John come to him in the hopes to become Amish, but he had made the effort to speak to him in the Old German. John couldn't have chosen a better phrase for the occasion, and Jacob could not deny John his dreams. Jacob resolved to speak to the other Amish, and begin John's training, "Yes, John. I am very pleased with your dedication to both Gott and my daughter. You shall be worthy of Sarah soon, so you may as well tell her of your intentions, before she sets eyes on another eligible bachelor," he chuckled. John had never seen Jacob smile before, let alone chuckle!

The next day, being Friday morning, John awoke at his normal time with his whole heart bursting with excitement. He wanted very badly to tell Sarah of the conversation that he and her father had had the night before, but he also wanted to choose just the perfect time to tell her. He had it thought out, and he hoped everything went according to plan. He would keep everything a secret from Sarah until tonight.

The day seemed endless to John, as he toiled away at his work. No matter how hot the day became, or how tired he felt, he felt an overwhelming sense of peace come over him, knowing he would eventually become a part of the community he had grown to love in such a short amount of time. Not only had he found a home and a new life filled with hope, he had also found the love of his life, who shared his love of music and singing. It filled him with absolute joy knowing that he was embarking on this new chapter in his life. As the sky darkened with the coming of dusk, John and Jacob stopped work. It was finally time for the family to have supper together. John's most favorite time of the day.

John explained to Jacob that he wanted to wash up and tidy himself before coming into the house for supper, so Jacob certainly sensed what was coming. He was happy for his daughter, but sad to lose her when she eventually married. Hope would have to take over the motherly duties of caring for her boppli bruder, but she had been well trained by her older sister.

Sarah served up the supper, and everyone took their place at the table. Everyone appeared to be hungry, and both her father and John remarked how delicious the chicken pot pie had turned out. She had handpicked the vegetables that she added to the chicken, and she did admit to herself that it tasted quite fresh and hearty. Right on schedule, Jacob excused himself saying that he was worn out. John helped with the cleaning up as he often did, and then Sarah helped put Hope and

Noah to bed, but not without singing a soft and heartwarming bedtime song of "Lavender's Blue." John closed his eyes as he listened to her angel voice. His mother had once sung him the very same lullaby when he was just a small child. It made him feel happy, yet sad that his mother would not get the chance to meet his beloved, or hear her wonderful singing voice.

Sarah emerged from the back bedroom, and joined John by the fire as was their new custom. John said he was feeling very tired, and that it was high time he got to bed, for tomorrow was Saturday, and there was much work to be done on the barn. He asked Sarah to walk with him, and so she did. John and Sarah strolled through the garden pathway towards his shack that had been transformed into a humble home. John said he had heard her singing the delicate lullaby to her sister and brother, and asked her to sing it once again for him as they sat down on the garden bench. Sarah was not surprised at his request, as she knew that John adored her singing. After she had finished the song, John got down upon his knee. Sarah could barely comprehend what was happening, since she was totally unaware of John's important conversation with her daed. John looked into Sarah's big brown eyes, and said what he had been waiting to say to her all night long,

"My dearest Sarah, I have taken the liberty to speak to your father about joining the Amish, and he has agreed that I shall begin my lessons this Sunday service. So, that being settled, I am now worthy of the question I am about to put to you. After my lessons have concluded, and I have become fully Amish, please be my wife. I must have you as my very own, and I shall want to hear you sing to our own future children the special lullaby you have just finished singing to me this night. I love you with all of my heart."

Sarah looked at him, her eyes welling with emotion, as she grabbed hold of his shoulders to hug him snugly in her arms,

"Yes, John, there is nothing in the world that would be more wonderful than becoming your wife! I have felt this since you first surprised me in daed's store."

And so, the two young lovers walked happily to John's little house, dreaming of their future together in the not so distant future...

Ephesians 5:19 "...speaking to one another with psalms, hymns, and songs from the Spirit. Sing and make music from your heart to the Lord..."

HANNAH

<u>**December**</u>

The service had been lovely as always but Hannah had been unable to concentrate, her mind bustling with dozens of thoughts. As she followed her fiancé's family from the home of one of the member and into the back area of their farm, she wrung her hands nervously.

"Hannah, are you unwell?" She jumped at the sound of Isaac's voice near her ear.

"Not at all! On the contrary, in fact," she replied, peering at him, confusion coloring her face. "What would make you ask such a thing?"

"You seemed not to be paying any attention whatsoever during the sermon. I believe the Bishop scowled at you at one moment." Shocked, Hannah paused in mid step to stare at her husband-to-be, abruptly holding up the line trekking through the field.

"You must be joking!" she cried and then saw the twinkle in Isaac's gentle hazel eyes.

"Perhaps I am but you must admit that your mind has been elsewhere today. What are you thinking about? I noticed the faraway look in your eye from my side of the room!" Hannah laughed and continued toward the barn where the Fisher family had arranged for lunch following their Sunday worship. The winter had been unseasonably warm and Hannah felt somewhat overdressed in her wool cloak. She wished for snow. It did not feel festive without snowflakes gracing the air.

"Well? What is it that plagues your thoughts? Are you reconsidering our marriage?" Again, Isaac's warm eyes lit up with laughter and Hannah grinned broadly at his jesting.

"Certainly not! I am simply concerned about Christmas," Hannah replied, her thoughts beginning to race once more. It was Isaac's turn to show confusion.

"What of Christmas? It is the loveliest time of year. Surely you can't be glum!"

"Not in the least," Hannah replied as they made their way into the spacious structure to join the rest of the congregation. "I am simply worried I have not prepared properly. I have made presents of all of the children and for my parents but I feel as though I have forgotten someone. Which brings me to the Christmas cards. I am always concerned that I have left out a family. Can you imagine how much embarrassment that would bring to us should I omit a single family? What's more is I set up the nativity scene in the front of our home and I cannot find one wise man and two angels. Now I suspect that Rachel has been playing with them but I have yet to find them and she denies knowing their whereabouts. I must have father whittle some for me or else it will be a disaster!"

Suddenly Hannah felt as though a huge weight had been lifted off her shoulders with the confession. Isaac burst into laughter.

"Oh, Hannah! The things which make you fret do amuse me endlessly. It is Christmastime, *liebchen*. It is not a time of worry and fret. That is for the English. We are only to give thanks and spend time with those dearest to us."

"I know, Isaac, but I cannot help wanting Christmas to be perfect! It is my favorite time of the year. And look! This year we haven't even any snow! It hardly seems proper to even set up a tree without the candlelight twinkling off the snow." Hannah pouted but immediately smiled as the truth of his words struck her. Of course he was right; this was not a time of stress. Their way was that of peace and order, not to be overshadowed by the trivialities which the outside word concerned themselves. It was what made the Amish community so special; the ability to block out the unnecessary and focus on the beauty of the basics in life. Hannah could not be happier. She and Isaac had become betrothed in February and their impending marriage was announced to the community in October as per tradition. They had plans to wed the following winter as per tradition and she could not have hoped for a better mate. Despite their engagement, Isaac continued to act as though they were newly enamored with one another, bequeathing her with beautiful flowers and penning poetry for her, words which made her warm to her soul. She was excited to begin her life with him. It seemed that the wedding was millennia away, not merely a year.

"Ah, Hannah, you may worry but your Christmas spirit is infectious," Bishop Philips told her, overhearing the last of their conversation. Blushing scarlet, Hannah turned to acknowledge him, bowing her head.

"Your sermon was well received today, Bishop," Hannah told him, trying to recover from her embarrassment. "It is a rare treat to hear you speak lately. I'm afraid we miss hearing your voice in service. I am pleasantly surprised you have joined us today."

"Unfortunately, I have had business in other districts as of late but I am happy to be back at home. I haven't had the opportunity to congratulate on your betrothal. Isaac, you have done well for yourself. The Yoder family is well respected in our district. Perhaps you will bless them with a son." The Bishop smiled at the couple.

"Not that the Yoder women are any less hard working than any of the men in our community. How is your family? I do not see your father here today," the Bishop continued, looking about, a sudden cloud covering his brown eyes. Hannah and Isaac followed his gaze. Hannah's mother, Ruth stood speaking with several other women while her sisters, Rachel and Miriam ran through the barn, playing a game of tag with some of the other children. As the three continued to look about, Hannah felt a stab of panic in her stomach. It was unheard of for her father, Mark to be absent from church services. She had spent the previous week in Isaac's district at a family member's home. Hannah had been slowly learning the workings of his father's farm at the insistence of Mark who thought it best she understood the complexities of her husband's land as much as possible. As Hannah's cousins resided in close proximity to Isaac's farm, the transition had been seamless and it allowed for their sweet courtship to continue uninterrupted. This also meant, however, that Hannah was not as informed as to the comings and goings of her own family. Brow furrowed, Hannah excused herself and hurried over to her mother, despite Isaac's reactionary hand on her arm to stop her.

"*Mamm*, where is *Daed*?" she whispered in her mother's ear urgently without preamble. Ruth gave Hannah a reproving look and politely exited the conversation in which she was involved.

"Mind your manners, Hannah!" Ruth Yoder chided her daughter.

"I'm sorry Mammi, I am just worried about him. It is unlike him to miss service. I can't recall one instance prior to this one in .fact!" Hannah insisted. Seeing her oldest daughter's distress, Ruth's face softened.

"Your father was away at market in Pittsburgh over the weekend. He was expecting to be back last night but the weather turned so he must have been detained. He will likely be home when we return." Hannah exhaled with relief and returned to her fiancé and the Bishop where she reiterated what she had been told. A bell rang to indicate that the meal was about to be served and they all sat at the long tables set up in the middle of building. Yet as they bowed their heads and grace was said, once again, Hannah felt herself distracted by unstoppable thoughts. This time, however, they were not of snowfalls and wise men. Suddenly she her mind was focussed completely on the whereabouts of her father.

"I don't mind, Hannah but I cannot help but feel you are overreacting somewhat," Isaac informed her as they pulled their carriage toward the Yoder farm.

"He is my father. I must know that he is well, Isaac," Hannah replied.

"*Liebchen*, he has been going to market since well before you were born. I am sure he is well. You will see." Isaac smiled boyishly at her and encouraged the horses onward. Hannah felt an uncharacteristic smidgen of annoyance at his placation. She gave him a sidelong look but said nothing. She hoped he was right but some inherent sense told her something was amiss. Inclement weather or not, Mark Yoder would have been at worship. His devotion to God was his priority, probably above his own health and safety. Hannah knew her father. He would have risked riding in a blizzard to honor his commitment to the community. Her mother had arrived back from the Miller farm with Rachel and Miriam and the pale afternoon light was already becoming dark, forsaking dusk altogether.

"I do not see his wagon," Hannah mumbled as they pulled to a stop. Alarm growing in her chest, Hannah recognized the Bishop's carriage which was parked behind the modest house. Hannah did not wait for Isaac to escort her from her seat and instead was running up the front steps to toward the door. As she flew inside the house, she stopped in her tracks. Her mother was on her knees, surrounded by Rachel and Miriam, a look of shock upon their faces. Tears had slipped from their cheeks to the wood floor. Bishop Phillips stood, solemn faced at the base of the stairs, his hat in his hands, his lips pursed into a fine line. They did not need to speak. Hannah already knew.

January

"Hannah, Isaac came calling again," Miriam told her, pushing open the door to the bedroom where her sister sat brushing her long hair, placing it into sections for braiding. Hannah did not respond. Instead she continued to count the strokes, slowly, meticulously smoothing down the strands.

"Hannah? Hannah!" Miriam strode into the room and snatched the utensil from her sister's grip. The older girl looked up in surprise and instinctively grabbed it back.

"What is it?" she demanded, rising to her feet menacingly.

"Isaac was here," Miriam said again. "He would like you to contact him when you are well."

"I am well, thank you. I am simply busy. With *Daed* in the hospital, fighting for his life, someone needs to help *Mamm* run the farm, Miriam. I cannot up and run off to help him when Isaac has able bodied brothers there. What does he want from me?" Her words were like a torrent of venom and twelve-year-old Miriam stepped back, shocked at her tone.

"I believe that he wants to know if you're well, Hannah. I don't think he wants you to help him on the farm," she offered, timidly, tears filling her eyes. Hannah was immediately contrite but her anger would not lessen.

"Thank you, Miriam. I will be in contact with Isaac shortly." Her sister immediately retreated from the bedroom, closing the door in her wake but Hannah heard her sister's stifled sob before she retreated down the stairs. Hannah knew that her tone had been unreasonably harsh but she could not seem to alleviate the insurmountable rage which had filled her since the horrendous accident her father had endured a mere month before. The driver who had injured Mark so severely on that lone road heading home from the city had yet to be caught and Hannah knew she would not rest until the person had been apprehended and brought to justice. Christmas had come and gone in an unmemorable blur, still filled with family and friends but in a much more somber tone than the joy of the season typically brought. The family had left the candles lit in the windows well after other members of the community had extinguished theirs, a constant flame for others to keep Mark in their prayers. Hannah remembered thinking that the nativity scene was ruined and she had reprimanded Rachel harshly for playing with the wooden characters, reducing the child to a blubbering mess. Much more than that, Hannah could not recall about holiday. There had been an exchange of gifts but Mark's had lay unopened at the hearth and Hannah did not have any recollection of what she had received. Hannah's mother had continued her duty, tending to the farm and caring for the children and Hannah had stepped in to assist as opposed to joining Isaac. At first, Isaac had attempted to stay nearby, offering his unselfish aide to the Yoder family but eventually Hannah's increasingly sullen behavior had driven him home to his family's land. Still, he had frequently visited his beloved to see how she was faring. More often than not, Hannah made herself unavailable for reasons no one could comprehend. While she never admitted it to anyone, she blamed Isaac also for her father's fate. *If only he had been more vigilante, heeded my words more carefully when I suggested that something was amiss with father,* she told herself time and again. It did not matter that Mark Yoder had been hit on the Saturday night, well before Hannah had any inkling that there was trouble. In Hannah's grief she was beyond reason and all she had remaining was her intense anger. It was irrelevant whom was the recipient of her rage. It needed to be released and Hannah ensured that it was so. Mark's initial prognosis had been grim. The internal damage to his organs was severe and he had several broken bones. He was still on a life support machine in the hospital where he had been taken following being struck. Hannah could not bear to see her strong, vital father in such a condition and had refused to attend his side despite her mother's pleading.

"Hannah, your father needs you there," Ruth had begged her daughter. "Please swallow your repulsion and spend some time at his side. He can hear your prayers."

"He can hear my prayers from here, Mamm. It makes not difference if I am here or there. I cannot bear to see him in such a state with wires poking out of him. Hospitals are filled with harsh lights and harsher people," Hannah countered. "I will not be any good to him there. He knows I am with him in spirit."

Any amount of argument had been futile and eventually Ruth gave up, attending the county hospital with only her two youngest.

"God will not allow him to be taken from us," Ruth assured Hannah one night, attempting to connect with her distraught oldest child.

"God should not have allowed him to have been struck in the first place!" Hannah had yelled back. "God should have been watching out for him. God should have rendered the driver comatose and on life support!"

There was no point in debating the issue. In her mind, Hannah would not rest until she saw the face of the person responsible for the atrocity writhing in shame, guilt and agony.

<u>February</u>

"Ma'am I understand your anger but there we are doing everything we can."

Hannah's blue eyes flashed but she checked her temper.

"Sir, it has been almost three months and you have absolutely no leads regarding the driver of the vehicle which struck my father. Surely you should be exploring other avenues to catch this animal! Doesn't it concern you that this kind of person is driving on your streets where your children walk?"

"Hannah!" Isaac gently placed his hand on her shoulder as she rose from her chair to confront the police detective at the desk. He turned apologetically to the detective.

"Hannah has been under a lot of stress since the accident," Isaac told the man who nodded understandingly.

"Of course, we fully get that and we sympathize," Detective Adams replied. "I have heard that your father is no longer on life support. We are all very happy to hear that."

Hannah felt her hands clench into fists, her nails digging into her palms.

"Yes, praise the Lord for small favors," she answered shortly, her eyes narrowing, ignoring Isaac's fingers which were now increasing pressure on her shoulder. "However, that does not change anything. Is this why nothing has been done to find the monster responsible? Because he is alive? Next time he may not be so lucky if this person is still on the road!"

"Miss Yoder, I assure you that we are doing everything we can but it is very difficult with the circumstances. There were no witnesses, it was a dark road..."

Hannah threw up her hands. She understood. Mark Yoder was not a priority to these people. He would have to be dead or English for them to care. They were just going to say words until she left them alone. Worried she would not be able to contain a barrage of words threatening to escape her lips, she turned to leave without responding. Hannah heard Isaac apologizing for her rudeness once more but Hannah did not wait for her fiancé. Moments later, he was at her side, breathing heavily from chasing her down the crowded street. Under normal circumstances, Hannah would have been unnerved by the throng of people in her midst. It was not like her to visit town, much preferring the quiet way of her community but it had been months and there had been no advancement regarding the driver who had struck her father. Against her mother's pleas, Hannah had taken it upon herself to meet with the detective face-to-face.

"Please, Hannah, Bishop Phillips has been in constant contact with the police. You must not go and bother them."

"If not me, then who?" Hannah had demanded.

"Go see your father! He needs you!" Ruth implored. But the words had fallen upon deaf ears and Ruth had summoned Isaac to accompany her now wayward daughter into town. Isaac had appeared as Hannah was setting off.

"Hannah! That was rude!" He breathed, struggling to keep up with her brisk stride.

"Well perhaps that's what they need, rudeness. Niceties don't seem to be getting us anywhere."

"Hannah, I'm sure they are doing everything they can – "

"It is not enough!" Hannah snapped. Isaac stopped walking, taken aback by her tone. Hannah had never had occasion to speak to him in such a manner. He watched after the woman he was destined to marry and he wondered what had happened to the gentle, even tempered girl he had courted. He understood she was frazzled, not acting rationally but deep down, he hoped that girl was not lost forever.

<u>March</u>

"Hannah, you have not been at worship in several weeks."

The statement was blunt but not filled with accusation. Bishop Phillips simply stared at her, his brown eyes wise with understanding. She shrugged nonchalantly and did not turn from the hens from which she was collecting eggs.

"God knows where I am," she responded flippantly. Bishop Phillips drew closer to her inside the coop, ignoring the squawking of the animals in his midst.

"It is not simply of God knowing where to find you," he told her, gently. "Worship is a place of community, a place where others can shoulder your burden while asking for the Lord's help."

Hannah reeled around to glare at him.

"What does the community know of shouldering my burden?" she asked. "Can they find the animal who ran down my father like a rabid dog in the street? Have they made him pay penance for the harm he has caused my family?"

A warm, fatherly hand reached her shoulder and the Bishop smiled weakly.

"Perhaps not, child, but your suffering is our suffering also. We grow together and we will support one another. That is what makes us strong. You cannot fight this burden alone."

"I am not alone," Hannah retorted. "I have my family. I have Isaac."

But even as she said the words, Hannah tried to remember the last time she had spent more than a few moments with her betrothed. She could not. She shoved the thought from her mind. It did not matter. The only importance was figuring out who had hurt her father. Isaac would have to understand that her priority was with her father.

<u>April</u>

"Hannah! Hannah!"

Miriam and Rachel's footsteps could be heard reverberating through her bedroom well before the door flew open and the twins appeared. Her heart in her throat, Hannah turned away from the window out of which she had been staring for well over an hour, lost in thought.

"What is it? Is it *Daed*? Is he dead?"

Shocked, the girls recoiled at her words, smiles fading from their lips.

"No!" Rachel cried. "Of course not! Why would you say such a thing?"

In truth, Hannah had been waiting for news of the like and had been since the day he had been hospitalized. Her heart began to slow and she forced herself to smile at her sisters.

"I'm sorry. What is it?"

"He's awake! *Daed* is awake!"

Hannah's slowing pulse picked up speed once more. She flung herself into her siblings' arms and the three rejoiced at the news.

"He is? When did this happen? What did the doctors say?" Hannah whipped the questions at them rapid fire. Ruth appeared in the doorway. Her face was gaunt from exhaustion and emotion.

"He will still need some time to recover in the hospital," Ruth answered. "But his ribs are healing as well as his kidneys." Hannah pulled away from the twins and looked at her mother, her face alight with excitement. *Now we will catch you! Daed will identify the driver and it will all be over!*

"Did he say anything?" she pressed. "Can he identify the driver? Or the vehicle? Does he know who hit him?"

Ruth's sky colored eyes clouded over and she regarded her daughter for a moment.

"Hannah, it is not healthy for you to focus so direly on the driver. God will sort out what to do with him. You must instead think of your father and concentrate on good thoughts." Hannah scowled at her mother.

"I am focussed on *Daed*! That is why I want to find out who did this to him! Why am I met with resistance at every turn? You, Isaac, Bishop Phillips. Am I the only one who cares about seeing justice served?"

Ruth pursed her lips together and did not reply. Hannah continued to stare at her mother.

"Well? What did he say? Did he identify the man or not?" she demanded. Ruth sighed heavily.

"No, Hannah. He cannot speak. He had a stroke."

May

Springtime held the promise of new birth for everyone in the community but Hannah. She found herself tending to chores indoor more and more. Isaac had ceased visiting altogether and Hannah found herself in the police station once a week, hounding Detective Adams mercilessly. Where the women in the community would have typically begun to make suggestions for her wedding, offering assistance and chattering cheerfully of their own nuptials, Hannah found herself almost isolated, something she was quite content in discovering. The feeling of helplessness which had overwhelmed her was becoming a suffocating blanket as more time passed and left her no closer to finding the heathen who had hurt her father. She still had not gone to the hospital to see Mark, despite reports from her family that he was faring quite well. He still had not managed to recoup his motor skills and Hannah did not want the face of a crippled man plaguing her already dark thoughts. She would not rest until someone had paid.

June

"You are attending service."

Her voice was flat and left no room for argument. Hannah opened her mouth to speak but caught the anger in her mother's usually gentle eyes and thought better of voicing her thoughts. Grudgingly, she retreated to her room to ready herself for worship.

The family hosting church services was a neighbor and the Yoder family arrived just as Bishop Phillips rose to speak. He fixated his eyes upon Hannah and began to preach of forgiveness. Hannah closed her ears and averted her eyes. *I will forgive when the driver asks for forgiveness. Not one moment before. And even then, I may not.*

July

He came home on a Tuesday and several members of the community were present to welcome Mark. They brought flowers and honey and bombarded him and the family with well wishes. Isaac and his family had driven in also but Hannah only watched the event from her bedroom window, unable to watch her enfeebled father slowly stumble his way up the steps of the veranda. Her eyes filled with tears but whether they were of guilt or pain, she was not sure. As Mark made his way inside with the help of his wife and two youngest daughters, Isaac lifted his eyes toward Hannah's bedroom window. His own eyes were filled with sadness and Hannah quickly ducked back behind the curtains, not willing to look at him. It had been a long while since they had spent time together and she admitted that she missed his company dearly. She often wondered what he was doing and if he thought of her. The look on his face told Hannah that he did long for her as she did him. Swallowing the urge to run downstairs and beg him for forgiveness, Hannah sat on the edge of the bed. She wondered if anything would ever be the same again.

August

"Hannah! Hannah!"

Rachel almost knocked Hannah over as she barreled into the barn. Hannah looked up at her quickly.

"What is it?"

"*Daed* said his first clear word!" Hannah felt hope swell in her chest.

"What did he say?" she asked, wiping her hands on her apron and following Rachel out of the building, toward the house.

"He said 'Hannah.' He's asking for you!"

September

Progress was swift from that moment onward. Every day, Mark Yoder began to say more. He was required to see a specialist in town to assist him in his walking but Hannah was beginning to see signs of the same, strapping man she had admired her whole life. She found it less painful to be in his presence but she still could not help but feel enraged at his condition. When Hannah did stay at his side, she pressed him for details of the accident. To her relief, he recalled a great deal and Hannah feverishly wrote down the details as Mark remembered, every day adding more to the description. Finally, after three weeks, she had a proper sketch of the vehicle and possibly the driver which she immediately took to the police station. *Now we've got you!* She thought smugly.

October

"Are we still to marry?"

The question startled Hannah as she had not heard Isaac at her back. He had been watching her from the porch as she hummed to herself, picking wildflowers. Oddly, the upcoming wedding had been fresh in her mind for the first time in months. Since delivering the description to the police, Hannah had felt as though they were nearing absolution and a giant weight seemed to have been lifted from her shoulders. She stared in surprise at her fiancé.

"I certainly hope so, Isaac. Are you reconsidering?" She felt faint as she waited for him to answer. Slowly, Isaac made his way down the steps and toward his betrothed.

"I feel as though we have become very distant these past months, Hannah. I wondered if you still wished for us to marry." She met the distance between them and offered him her hands.

"Forgive me, Isaac! I have been consumed with worry for my father. Of course I have never thought for a moment that you and I would not be wed." Isaac eagerly accepted her hands and squeezed them gently, smiling with relief.

"I am glad you have finally decided to forgive and move on," he told her. "I knew the sensible woman I know was in there somewhere."

Hannah beamed back at him.

"It will be very easy to move on once this man is caught! I believe the police will finally catch him now!"

The smile died on Isaac's lips as he stared at Hannah. He realized that she was still consumed with the idea of catching the driver. Wisely, he said nothing but a sense of unease filled his stomach. Would this never end?

<u>November</u>

"You must be very excited with the upcoming wedding, Hannah. It has been quite a year for you and your family. It will be a relief to have cause for celebration over bad times, I would say," Bishop Phillips said after service. Hannah smiled widely and nodded, glancing at Isaac. He smiled meekly.

"Yes, we are looking forward to it. A Christmas wedding may seem a bit ostentatious but it is my favorite time of year and Isaac has been kind enough to indulge my whimsy on this matter," Hannah answered happily.

"Well I think it is a wonderful idea. It will only solidify your union with Christ. I am happy to see your father up and about."

"Yes, he is already back into manning the farm as he was prior to the accident."

"Well that is wonderful news, Hannah. It must certainly alleviate your desire to see the perpetrator arrested. It was not good for you to be so fixated on such negative thoughts for so long," the Bishop told her, turning to nod at other members of the congregation.

"No, Bishop, I can focus on other things now. The police are closing in on the animal now that my father has given them somewhere to look. We will have our justice in due time. I must leave it in their hands now." The Bishop looked at Hannah sharply.

"Your father knows who hit him?"

"He gave a very accurate description of the man, yes," Hannah replied. "But as you say, Bishop, it is in God's hands now. I have decided to focus more on my husband-to-be and deal with the criminal when he is found."

Bishop Phillips nodded, his eyes dark.

"Yes, it is in God's hands," he agreed.

December

The police were standing on her porch and Hannah felt her heart leap into her throat.

"Miss Yoder? Is your father home?" the detective asked her, peering over her shoulder. She nodded eagerly and granted them entry. Mark sat in a rocking chair in the front room. He rose to his feet with an agility he did not possess even two weeks prior.

"Please do come in, officers," he told them, cordially. Awkwardly, the detectives ventured into the humble home and stood in the doorway.

"Have you found the man responsible?" Hannah demanded. "Is that why you're here?"

Mark gave her a reproachful look.

"Hannah, where are your manners? Would you like a beverage?" Both men shook their heads and fidgeted nervously.

"Well?" Hannah demanded when there was silence. "Have you news?"

"Hannah!" Mark chided again but the lead detective held up his hand and nodded.

"Yes, Miss Yoder. We have your man. Someone has turned himself in."

Hannah's face went through a variety of changes; hope, shock and then anger.

"He turned himself in?" she almost yelled. "After one year? What kind of monster lets a family suffer for an entire year before confessing his crime?"

"Hannah..."

"Yes, Miss Yoder but frankly, in these situations, it is extremely difficult to find hit and run drivers. We are very lucky that someone did come forward at all," the policeman interjected. "But I do understand your frustration."

"I doubt it," Hannah mumbled. "Where is he?"

"He is in the county lock up. We would like your father to come with us to see if he can be identified in a line up but he had fully confessed to the accident."

"Who is he? A young, drunk English boy?" Hannah asked contemptuously, already envisioning the short haired punk, smoking a marijuana cigarette. Again, an uncomfortable silence ensued. Hannah stared at the men expectantly.

"Who is he?"

Detective Adams cleared his throat.

"It is someone you know," he said evasively. Hannah exchanged concerned looks with her father.

"Who?" she pressed.

"He is your Bishop. Daniel Phillips."

"Hello Hannah."

Hannah felt her legs turn to jelly as she stared at her much-loved Bishop behind the bars of the county jail.

"It is true," she whispered. "How did this happen?"

"I wish I could explain it to you, child but there is nothing I can say which will take away what you and your family have endured over this year."

"Please tell me what happened," she begged, her eyes filled with tears. The Bishop took a breath and told her the story he had relived in his head over and over since the day it had happened.

He had travelled the road hundreds, if not thousands of times before but Bishop Phillips had not slept more than two hours a night in over three weeks. There had been minor unrest in two of the neighboring districts, some petty squabbling which should have resolved itself but somehow a miniscule issue had become a weeks long debate. He was grateful that he was finally able to return home to his district. The car in which he rode had been a gift from a Bishop in one of the districts who had taken pity upon his constant state of commute. Bishop Phillips had to admit that it was more luxurious than his hard riding horse and cart but he also knew that he should not get too attached.

As the headlights lit the way around the road, his heart leapt into his throat. A doe stood frozen in the road, shocked by the onset. In his exhaustion, it took a few seconds for his reaction time to match up with his vision. He slammed on the brakes and veered to the left of the road, barely grazing the tail of the animal but full on impacting something else; a horse drawn cart. The mare whinnied in pain and shock as the Bishop struggled to steady the still moving vehicle. As all was still, Bishop Phillips opened the door to the car and ran toward the now toppled buggy. Inside lay the still body of Mark Yoder, seemingly lifeless. Bishop Phillips stood stock still, unsure of what to do. I must stay and wait for help, he told himself. Then he remembered the two glasses of wine he had consumed with supper. Slowly, he backed up and slipped back into the car, driving away undetected into the black night.

Tears fell from her lids onto her cheeks as she looked at the broken man before her. She thought of how badly she had wanted him to suffer but all she could think of was how much he had already suffered. He must have wanted to ease her agony a thousand times but had been trapped in his own nightmare.

"I understand that you must loathe me, Hannah. You have every right to feel as such," Bishop Phillips told her, his voice cracking. Gently, Hannah reached between the bars and offered the Bishop her hands. He grabbed them instantly and looked at her pleadingly.

"I forgive you," she said simply.

Christmas

"Oh, Hannah you look beautiful," Ruth told her daughter, embracing her warmly. "I have been looking forward to this for so long!"

Hannah laughed.

"Yes, me too Mammi," she joked and lovingly returned her mother's caress. She looked at herself in the mirror one last time. She vowed to her reflection that with this new start she would forsake all anger and rely on God to give her strength in the worst of times. She knew how fortunate she was that Isaac had been strong enough to stand by her during such a trying time and she would never forget it. She turned and looked at her mother and sisters.

"Are you ready?" Miriam asked, hopping back and forth from one foot to another. Hannah looked around and suddenly her stomach dropped.

"Where is *Daed*?" she asked, feeling a familiar sense of panic seize her. The curtain was quickly drawn and Mark strolled in, his gait strong and perfect.

"I am here, *liebchen*. Do you think I would miss giving away my oldest daughter?" he answered. His voice was slightly slower than it had been but his words were perfectly pronounced. There was no sign of the stroke he had suffered. Hannah exhaled. Everything was right again.

BE GOOD, MY STARLIGHT : AN AMISH ROMANCE
NATALIE SALEM

Chapter One

"Be good, my starlight, I love you," Naomi said gently. She leaned down and hugged her son tight. He was just barely five, but was now old enough to start classes.

His golden hair looked nothing like her brown locks, his brown eyes were so dark compared to her green ones. He was hers, though, despite appearances. He was her entire world, and she knew that she'd do anything to make sure he was happy and unaware of the hardships she faced. He kissed her cheek, and then immediately ran off with a couple other boys to start their lessons.

Her family was setting her up with a stranger.

He was supposedly a good man.

Naomi was yet to see that, she knew that he'd be at her home with her family by the time she returned from her son's school. She knew he was a hard worker, that he had a daughter, and that he was ten years older than her.

She wasn't keen on him being thirty, but she knew that, given her circumstances, he was starting to look like the only option.

Naomi looked back at the school house as she started back home. The elderly teacher, Mister Lapp, was ushering in the last of the children, and she watched him with interest.

He had a job in this community.

A place.

Nobody would look at him and wonder why he was alone, or who he was.

She wished for a life so easy.

The soft summer grass gave way under her shoes as she headed back to the main street. Golden light, radiating off a bright morning sun, brought her entire village to life and motion around her.

Everyone was pleased to greet one another, everyone was starting their day and jobs.

Except her.

Nobody greeted her as she walked through the village, she kept her eyes averted in fear of any stray staring. She felt like how she imagined English must feel when they come into town with their shiny cars.

Different.

Unwanted.

She tried to distract herself, and remind herself of things she knew of Vernon.

He was 30, owned land as a farmer, was a widower. He had a daughter who was nearing seven and was in desperate need of a mother since she'd be out of school within the next handful of years.

Vernon sounded respectable.

Sounded like her only chance.

Still, as Naomi reached her family's home, she couldn't help but feel a pang of regret. A marriage without love wasn't much of a marriage. A marriage of convenience would help her family, help her reputation, help her life, but she'd still hurt. She'd still feel out of place and unhappy. She was sure of it. Naomi let herself in, pulled off her black bonnet, and reassured herself that this would be fine: she needed to think of her family and son first.

"Naomi, are you home?" her father called from the kitchen. She could smell that her mother was cooking something, despite the fact that they all just had breakfast.

"I am, father," she replied, following his voice. The kitchen was large, but as she walked in, and felt all eyes upon her, it felt very tight and small.

A man she'd never seen before was standing in the corner sipping what smelled like very dark coffee. He was taller than her, his face shaven to show he was unmarried. She noted that he was handsome, that he looked sturdy and strong, but she felt no strong pull to him.

"This is Vernon Miller," her father introduced, motioning to the man. "We were talking about the idea of marriage between you two," he said flatly.

Naomi felt her heart drop.

She knew that this was her family's goal, but she'd thought she'd been given the chance to court first. She looked to her mother for help, but her mother just cast her eyes aside and turned back to cooking.

"It's good to meet you," Vernon said, standing and offering his hand to her. The action felt incredibly intimate, given what was just said, but she took his hand and shook it softly anyways. His grip was firm, his hand was warm.

She didn't want this.

Still, she knew better than to be rude.

"Nice to meet you as well," she replied.

"Can I drive you home from church on Sunday?" he offered. Naomi almost laughed, that was the kind of courting only teenagers did, and he was almost twice the age he should be to ask.

Her father gave her a stern look, though.

"I would like that," she replied. "Would you like more coffee?"

"I would be very thankful for more," he answered, not taking his eyes off of hers. A blush flooded her cheeks from the attention, and Naomi quickly took his mug to get out of his sight.

He talked with her father comfortably about the farm work, about how much land he owned. It discomforted her to realize he was the same space in age from her parents as he was to her. She couldn't imagine her mother or father marrying someone so much younger than they were.

Naomi gave him his coffee, and he stopped to spare her a smile before he continued talking. He was trying harder to impress her parents than he was to impress her, she didn't mind. She was almost complemented to think that he actually wanted her.

Soon he was leaving, and she was set to work in the garden to keep it weeded and watered.

She was sure if she set her mind to it she could love him.

She was 20, the age most girls would be able to choose if they wanted to leave the church or not. The age most women would have dozens of offers and freedom to choose as they wished.

Yet she had to scramble and grab to get the one offer she did.

Her family loved her, cared about her, and they were trying to make sure that she lived happily. They didn't want to see her grow old and alone, with just her son in her life.

They didn't want her to have to spend her entire life in their home.

A plane passed overhead, and Naomi craned her neck and let herself watch it. She couldn't help but wonder, if her situation had been different and she were English instead, would she have been happier with that life?

She'd had the choice taken from her, though.

Naomi had sworn to the church and was going to live her whole life happily being a part of it.

She loved her son, John, would do anything to protect him and raise him well. She'd fallen pregnant with him at just fifteen.

Fallen from grace in the community when she gave birth to him at age fifteen.

She'd had many friends, had a fun life, before her pregnancy.

She'd gone to sings to meet boys, had been courted by two, and yet one poor decision had left her ostracized from everyone but family.

Sighing as the plane went out of sight, Naomi felt resigned.

She'd make herself fall in love with him.

Almost six years since she was found to be pregnant had passed, almost six years she had spent unwanted.

He wanted her.

He was interested in her.

She couldn't see herself getting another chance like this, and she didn't want to let down her family.

She'd love him eventually, she was sure of it.

Chapter Two

The next day, a bright and sunny Tuesday, Naomi and her son arrived to the school to find it closed. A sign hung on the door, white crisp paper with clear handwriting. When she could finally get close enough, through the gaggle of mothers and children reading it, she was shocked.

Mister Lapp, the elderly school teacher, had passed in the night from a heart attack.

Naomi walked John home, disturbed and unsure of how to explain it to him. He didn't have to deal with death yet, her parents, and her parent's parents, were all alive still.

She hadn't expected him to pass, then again she never really saw death coming for anyone. Once someone got to a certain age they moved back in with one of their children to live out their retirement in comfort. Most people didn't work until they died.

The rest of her day was spent more heavily considering marrying Vernon. If she passed he would be much more able to take care of her son than her aging parents or her two older siblings who had left the church.

The next day, despite her heart telling her the school would still be closed, she walked her son the same path she did most days.

Nobody else with children were about, nobody seemed to be heading to the school. She felt foolish at first, before realizing someone was in the school house.

The sign was gone from the door.

"Hello?" she asked, holding her son's hand as she peeked inside the schoolhouse doors. There was a young man at the front of the classroom, flipping through a book. He looked up at the sound of her voice and smiled.

"Hello! Please, come in," he said, motioning to her and John. She couldn't help but notice the rest of the room was empty besides them, usually there were at least twenty children in class every day.

"Where is everyone?" she asked, surprised.

"I was just asking myself the same question," he smiled sadly, looking pointedly around. "They may be taking a day to grieve," he offered as an explanation.

"Must be," she murmured, trying not to notice how handsome the man was. He had a strong jawline, but sweet blue eyes. His cheekbones were sharp, and they led her attention to his soft looking lips. His face was clean shaven. Unmarried.

His looks were hard to ignore.

"I'll call it an off day, then," he sighed, leaning back against his desk.

"Are you from the area?" she found herself asking. She was sure she'd know if she'd seen him before. He was too attractive to be forgettable, and too close-looking to her age for him to have not been to the same sings and gatherings as her.

"I've been caught," he joked. He was lighthearted, warm. She was caught off guard and found herself savoring it. Not many people in her village even acted like she existed anymore. Years of shame had left her starving for any kind of positive attention. "I'm from a town in Idaho, I wanted a move to see what the rest of our churches had to offer," he explained.

"Have you taught before?"

"Mommy can we go?" her son interrupted before the new man could answer.

"John, I need you to have patience," she said softly, leaning down to his height. He looked slightly scolded, but sat down in one of the chairs and waited.

"He's so well behaved," the new teacher said, watching him.

"Thank you," she said gently. A child who misbehaved was a bad mark on the parent and she knew it. A compliment on her son was a compliment to her.

"Of course," he replied. "I'm Eli," he walked towards her, offering his hand.

"Naomi," she said softly, accepting his hand and shaking it. She felt shocks go through her body at the contact. What was this feeling?

He let go of her hand slowly, and she immediately missed the contact.

"I taught grades kindergarten through third for a year in Idaho," he said, answering the question she'd asked earlier.

"I see," Naomi made herself answer.

She wanted to say more, to ask more, but she forced herself to have some control.

"We should go," she said after a moment, looking down at her son who was starting to drift off to sleep. "Thank you, I'll make sure word gets out that there will be class tomorrow," she said gently, smiling.

"That would be very kind," he smiled. "Have a good day," he offered.

"You also," she nodded, leading her son out.

She'd found him attractive.

More than that, she corrected herself, she was attracted to him.

Quietly she admonished herself as they headed back to her parent's home. She knew better than to seek the attention of men. She knew that it never worked out well for her.

Yet she found herself glancing back at the schoolhouse to see if she could catch a glimpse of the new teacher.

He was looking out the window back at them.

Color fled onto her cheeks and she looked back towards their path. He was handsome, educated. He had a job that would leave him being an important part of the community.

Eli.

She repeated his name in her mind.

It was a common name, but it felt special attached to him. She regretted not learning his last name, and as she had this thought more guilt fled her heart.

If he knew anything about her.

About her situation.

He wouldn't have been so sweet to her, she was sure of it.

Eli was kind because he was a teacher, because it was his job to be, not because he was interested in her. She took a deep breath and reminded herself that her family had picked a very suitable man for her anyways.

This was just cold feet.

Her family had laid a very straight line for her, and if she followed it she could be very happy.

Vernon was an older man, but he had lived there his whole life, had roots in the community. Eli was attractive and closer to her age, but he would want to start from scratch with a respectable wife.

Not with her.

Naomi scooped up her son and carried him the rest of the way home in her arms, trying not to admit to herself how excited she was to see Eli the next day.

Chapter Three

The next morning there were many people at the school.

Eli was talking, and smiling, and being more than friendly with the other mothers who had come. Naomi took it as confirmation that he really was just being nice to her.

She didn't need to read into him too much.

Tightening her bonnet a little she walked John the rest of the way to the school.

"Miss Naomi," he greeted her, his smile warm and welcoming.

"I don't think I caught your last name," she replied, also smiling.

"Troyer," he answered, a friendly sound in his voice.

"Do take care of my boy, Mister Troyer," she said softly.

"He won't be too much trouble," Eli replied, shaking his head and smiling.

Naomi spent the rest of the walk home memorizing his smile.

That evening she got to thank him for his care, again.

His face stayed in her mind.

"You're smiling a lot today," he mother commented, the water on the stove started to boil. "Is it that you're keen to the idea of Mister Miller now?" she asked. There were no notes of teasing in her voice, it was an honest question.

"I'm keen to the idea of marriage," Naomi replied, keeping her answer vague.

She didn't want her mother to know.

The next day was Friday.

She tried to make excuses for herself as to why they were arriving at the school house a full twenty minutes later. The warm muffins in her basket were enough evidence to prove them all wrong.

"Mister Troyer?" she knocked on the schoolhouse door and peeked in. He was looking through papers at his desk. At their intrusion he glanced at the wind-up clock on his desk.

"You're early," he said, it wasn't accusing or confused, he was almost pleased sounding.

"I thought I'd welcome you properly to the community," she offered, bringing forward the muffins.

"They smell very good, thank you," he said, standing to meet them halfway to the door.

"Sorry about being so early, I was up early this morning and lost track of my time," she apologized as he accepted the basket.

"No, please, you're fine," he replied, shaking his head. "I haven't eaten today and these are a welcome sight," he added.

She went home that day feeling like she was floating.

Friday turned into Saturday, and then soon it was Sunday and Vernon was greeting her at church.

She'd almost forgotten about him.

Now, after she'd spent so many days getting glimpses and small moments with Eli at the schoolhouse, Vernon seemed very different to her.

He was older, more of a man. She knew thirty wasn't old by any standards, but Eli was her age. Vernon seemed more stern suddenly, and less interesting. He nodded to her, cordially, properly, and then she sat with her family.

The service was a memorial to Mister Lappe, the school teacher.

Guilt flooded Naomi again, it was her norm. She'd not mourned the teacher, she was too busy being interested in the new one.

In Eli.

In her interest and attraction, she'd lost her morals.

Naomi bowed her head, listening to the sermon, and started to pray for forgiveness. Regardless of how lonely she'd been, she didn't need to become selfish and thoughtless.

Vernon was an actual choice.

Her only choice.

Whatever she was thinking was interest from Eli was nothing more than courtesy from a teacher to his student's parent. She knew this, she needed to keep it in mind. If he knew anything about her, if he had the slightest inkling about how the town viewed her, he wouldn't be so friendly.

Flirting towards him, paying him any attention, was empty and useless.

She needed to get that through her head.

Newly resigned, she sat through the rest of the service and listened carefully. When church finally wound down to an end her family left her behind without mention, leading a sleepy John away for a nap. Naomi wished she could go with them and not have to talk to Vernon.

He appeared to her through the crowd, a small smile on his mouth, and she followed him to his buggy. Vernon was thoughtful, helping her up into the buggy, carrying on comfortable conversation about her family and his work.

He was sweet.

It made it worse.

She couldn't help but feel like if he were rude, if there was anything about him that she didn't like, she'd have an out.

He gave her no excuses.

He was kind, gentle, understanding. He was everything that, before knowing Eli, she would have wanted in a man. Her family had a keen eye in choosing him to be introduced to her, and she appreciated that. She wished he held her interest as well as Eli had.

"Your mother invited me for dinner Tuesday night," he said idly as they neared her home. "I wanted to check that you also want me there," he added, turning to her.

"We would all love to have you there," she said, not meaning it.

Her parents would love to have him there, and she would love to make her parents happy, regardless of what that meant for her.

Chapter Four

Monday came and Naomi didn't pause to greet Eli. She didn't make eye contact with him or smile to him as she dropped off her son.

She'd convinced herself that if she was going to rid herself of affection for him, the best way to do it was to stop letting herself talk warmly to him. Any interaction would be too much, and she wouldn't let it happen.

At least, she thought she wouldn't.

Six hours later, when she returned to pick up John, Eli asked her to stay after the class cleared out. She agreed to, feeling her heart race as he said her name. She beat down the feelings, but they just simmered under the surface instead. Her traitorous heart didn't care about what was right or pure, it just wanted his attention.

"Has John done something wrong?" she asked as the last of the children left with their mothers.

"No, never, he's a model student," Eli replied, shaking his head. He gathered the papers his students had left behind from their desks. "May I step outside with you while he stays in here?" Eli asked, making eye contact with her. His expression was apologetic, and her heart warmed over it.

She adored him.

"Did I anger you?" he asked as they stepped out. The day was overcast, the strong winds above pushed the clouds at an alarmingly high speed. There would be a storm by morning.

"No," she was honest.

"Are you well?" he asked, he was obviously concerned. She needed to clear the air or it would torture her forever. If she just leapt to Vernon's side as his wife without ever knowing if there was a chance with Eli, she'd never forgive herself.

"Why do you pay me attention?" she asked, the words tumbled out of her mouth like heavy stones.

He looked taken aback for just a moment. "I find you interesting, you're very kind and I want to return the favor," he answered.

"Nothing more?" she asked, unsure. His expression faltered for a moment.

"That's not entirely true," he sighed, leaning against the schoolhouse. He glanced in to look at John for a moment. "I find my thoughts stay with you even when you're not here," he admitted. "At first, I pushed it aside because I assumed you were married because of John," he said. "One of the other mothers mentioned you were single and lived with your parents, so I felt no guilt in talking to you."

"Even with a child out of wedlock?" she asked.

He looked uneasy for a moment. "It's something I would have to heavily consider before courting you."

"You'd consider courting me?" Naomi was even more surprised by this bit of information.

"I would at some point," he said, honestly. She read it as a 'no' since it wasn't a 'yes.

"I don't mean to make you uncomfortable," she replied, her heart dropping into her stomach. "I just," she sighed. "I misunderstood your intentions and I'm terribly sorry."

"Don't be," Eli said, shaking his head. "I'm not sure what I feel for you, I need to reflect and pray on it, can you give me a week?" he asked, his eyes were warm and sweet.

"Of course, take your time," Naomi answered, as if she weren't being rushed to marry Vernon.

She gathered John and they left.

John was happy to talk about how much he enjoyed Eli's lessons better, that they were more interesting than how Mister Lapp had taught them. Naomi scolded him for speaking ill of someone, if if they're dead, but was pleased to know her son took a shining to Eli. He hadn't even shown a little bit of interest in Vernon.

Tuesday morning when she took her son to school, she didn't talk to Eli or make eye contact with him. It was the same when she picked her son up after.

She didn't want to seem like she was trying to seduce him, didn't want to sway Eli into something he didn't want.

That night, Vernon was at their home for dinner. He and her father spoke about the weather, and of crops for the year. Naomi tried to pay attention and be as sweet and appealing as possible.

He could never know that she was on the verge of crying because of another man. It would just add more shame to who she was. Her mother stopped before cleaning dishes to invite him for dinner on Friday as well, and he accepted.

Her parents were getting her further and further into this man's life.

What would happen if by some miracle Eli accepted her and they started courting? Would her parents hate her for yanking them around?

Would they ever forgive her?

Nightfall found her sobbing in the garden after she set John to bed. Crickets filled the air with their noise, and she tried to distract herself with them.

She's only fallen pregnant with John because she'd kept secrets from her parents. She fell in love with a boy, and he tried to introduce her to all that he knew of the English. How wild and adventurous their lives could be, how different it was from their own world.

Naomi became swept up in those ideas.

She went further with him, becoming intimate, not entirely knowing what she was doing. Her mother had only ever said, "never take your dress off around anyone else,".

She fell pregnant.

Then, during the boy's Rumspringa, he'd left.

Left the church, left his family, left her.

Her parents were furious, they had expected him to marry her and be forced into staying with the church- but they couldn't take that choice away from him.

He left.

She never got to fully enjoy her Rumspringa because of him.

Never got to finish being young.

She was forced immediately into motherhood, into following that path, before she even got to see the world outside of her community. The people around her looked down on her for being a single mother so young, she felt every glare and sneer that had struck her over the last five years. Her shame was too painful.

All of this because she kept a secret from her parents.

Naomi wiped her face, but the tears kept falling.

"Naomi, what is it?" her mother's soft voice said from behind. Naomi jumped a little, startled, but then began to cry more at the sight of her.

"I think I love another man, mother," she explained. "He's considering courting me, and asked a week to think it over," she confessed it quickly, the words poured out of her like water.

"Why didn't you tell me?" her mother asked, sitting beside her she wrapped her arm around Naomi.

"I'm worried I'm being selfish again," she answered. Her mother didn't respond immediately, just sat their and held her softly.

"He sounds like a thoughtful man for waiting to think about it, and you sound like you've been thinking it over too," her mother answered. "I'll ask your father to tell Mister Miller to come next week instead of Friday, and if this other man asks to court you, we'll consider him instead," she explained.

"Are you sure?" Naomi asked, wiping her face.

"We just want you to be married and happy like we are, that's all," her mother explained.

"Thank you," Naomi sighed, ready and hopeful for Eli to give her an answer.

The rest of the week slid by like thick tar.

She tried to avoid looking at him at all, but kept catching her eyes flicking over to him and watching him. She wasn't happy that she had to see him twice a day, and started dreading taking John to and from school. Every time she saw Eli and he didn't approach her with an answer it felt like a more definite 'no'.

Sunday came, and he'd still not said anything.

Vernon offered to drive her home, and she let him, but she didn't say a word the whole way home. He didn't seem to notice. Unlike Eli, who immediately pointed out that she was acting odd, Vernon just kept talking about how he wanted to raise a new barn.

She was exhausted of him, and was starting to loathe how secure he seemed in marrying her.

***

Finally, it was Monday morning.

She wore her black bonnet, and her favorite dress and cape.

It wasn't flashy. Nothing she, or anyone around her, wore was, but it was her favorite shade of blue, and she felt lovely in it. She left early with John, so that Eli wouldn't have to say anything in front of anyone, and tried to keep a lid on her energy.

When she arrived he was behind his desk, writing.

"Sorry we're early, is it alright if I leave him here?" she asked. These were the first words she'd said to him in a week.

"That's fine," he answered, barely looking up from his papers.

It was a no, then.

Naomi nodded, then turned and bit her lip as she started to walk home. He didn't want to court her. Eli had no interest in her. Her heart ached, and she tried to remind herself that she still had Vernon as a possibility, she wouldn't be alone.

Somehow, that made it worse.

Chapter Five

She didn't tell her mother his answer when she got home.

She didn't start the laundry, like she did every Monday. She didn't do anything but go to her room and kneel to pray.

Naomi wanted answers.

She needed to know what to do next, where to take her path. Should she just give up on any other men and marry Vernon now that he was the only choice? Should she stay single and hope another eventually notices her?

Both options sounded terrible, but they were her only two.

The way he didn't even look her in the face burned at her heart again, and she started praying harder, looking for guidance between her tears. She didn't want to be alone for the rest of her life, but she also didn't want to end up in a loveless marriage. Her week of talking to and falling for Eli had been so warm and good, and although it was short lived she wanted to feel that way more. She wanted to feel loved.

Her mother came in to gather the sheets, starting the laundry since Naomi hadn't yet, and paused for a moment.

"It's been a week, today, and I think his answer is 'no,'" Naomi explained, standing up from kneeling.

"Then it's a blessing you also have Vernon in your life," her mother said, patting Naomi's hair softly for a moment, like she did when her daughter was younger. "We love you and will be here for you for as long as you want us," her mother explained.

Naomi knew that wouldn't last forever.

Her mother would need to retire eventually, would need someone to take care of her and offer her a home. Both of Naomi's older siblings left the church and wouldn't be able to offer that. If Naomi stayed single there was no way she could support them.

She'd have to marry Vernon. Marrying him was the only way to be sure that she could properly thank them for all they'd done for her. The only way to show God, and the church, that she truly was thankful for all she had.

"Tomorrow I'll tell father I'll marry Vernon if he'll have me. Today my heart needs to mourn," Naomi said, hugging her mother close.

"We're proud of you Naomi," her mother said. "We love you and John, we're glad to have you in our home," she explained.

Naomi cleaned her face and then set to helping with the laundry, letting it distract her.

The day passed more quickly now, and she almost lost track of the time. An hour before she was supposed to leave to pick John up from school, her son came running out to the garden to her.

"John! What are you doing here?" she asked, alarmed.

"Mister Troyer let us out early," he answered, hugging against her leg.

"Who walked you home?" she leaned down and looked him over, ensuring he was fine. His golden hair was so much like Eli's that she could almost see him as his son.

"Mister Troyer," he answered. "He told all the others that it was a short day," he went on. Then John began to babble about a math problem he was able to solve, but Naomi was completely distracted.

Why hadn't he told her it was a short day?

Why did he walk her son home?

Naomi stood quickly, looking over her dress and making sure that the soap hadn't soaked it. Taking John's hand in hers, she headed back into her parent's home.

There were voices in the main room of the house, and she followed through the kitchen to them.

Eli was sitting on a couch opposite her parents, and was talking to them comfortably. Naomi's heart was beating out of her chest, suddenly and strong.

He was here.

He was here and smiling at her.

She smiled back chastely, remembering herself, and sat down beside her mother. John kissed her goodbye and ran off to his room to do his homework.

"I want to court your daughter," Eli said flatly. "I know that usually this is done in other ways, that it would be kept quietly, but I learned this last week that Vernon was wanting her hand, and so I don't have the option to stay quiet." He watched over her parents carefully. The words caught Naomi by surprise and her whole body felt like it was buzzing.

He wanted to court her! She'd been resigned to being stuck marrying Vernon for her parent's future security, and now here was Eli. She knew she could so easily love him, she was already most of the way there, and they'd be happy together.

Naomi's mother exchanged a look with her, as if confirming this was the man she had cried over. When Naomi nodded, her mother turned to Naomi's father and murmured something softly to him.

His demeanor changed just slightly into a softer one.

"Do you own land?" her father asked, sitting back in his seat.

"I do, it has a home on it and room for a garden," Eli replied.

"Would your end intent be marriage?" her father asked. Naomi's heart pounded at the question.

"It would be," Eli didn't hesitate in saying his.

Naomi's heart was soaring. She tried to remember what prayers she had said before so that she could thank God for answering each of them. She wanted so much to just walk across the room and kiss Eli and say that she wanted the same.

The room was quiet, though.

She began to realize it had been a couple minutes since Eli answered, and her father still hadn't said anything. She turned to look at her father, gray seeping into his once-red beard, and watched his expression. He looked like he was seriously considering things.

"I see no problem in it," her father answered finally, breathing out slowly. "Just be true to her," he added.

"I will be," Eli replied.

He stayed a little longer and spoke casually with her father, looking over to Naomi every few moments like she was made of the stars themselves.

Nightfall began to near, and her mother offered for him to stay for dinner, but he declined and said he had to go over the tests.

"Naomi will walk you out then," her father said, heading to the kitchen with his wife.

Naomi's cheeks colored at the idea that her parents were leaving them alone. They stood together and headed to the front door slowly, their arms brushing.

"I'm sorry I didn't talk to you properly this morning," he said as they walked. "I was nervous to say it, to let it out, but I needed your family's permission first," he explained. "If I had spoken to you for more than a second I would have asked you to court me," he said, he was almost laughing.

"I'm so pleased you want to court me," it felt like an understatement, but she had to say something. "I like you very much," she admitted. They stood there, comfortable in each others silence, for a couple minutes as the evening's crickets began to pick up.

"I look forward to seeing you in the morning," he said gently, turning to her. "I always do," a smile was on his mouth.

"I do also," she replied.

He leaned towards her, and she met him halfway.

The kiss was gentle and sweet. His lips sent sparks through hers and in that moment she could see their future together.

A marriage with love.

Everything she'd ever wanted.

END

www.ingramcontent.com/pod-product-compliance
Lightning Source LLC
Chambersburg PA
CBHW031450130726

47989CB00003B/1334